ALSO BY LIZ ALDEN

The Love and Wanderlust Series

The Night in Lover's Bay (free prequel short story)

The Fling in Panama

The Slow Burn in Polynesia

The Second Chance in the Mediterranean

The Rival in South Africa (standalone novella)

The Player in New Zealand

The Best Friend in Indonesia (free standalone short story)

Aged Like Fine Wine Series

Rosé with My Fake Fiancé

Riesling with My Roommate

Prosecco with My Professor

Cava with My Colleague

Winter Wanderlust Series

Nutcracker with Benefits

Frosty Proximity

Ghost of Ex-mas Past

Run, Run, Roommates

Wanderlust Resort Series

Beach Boss (free standalone short story)

Beach Resolution

Put it in Beach Mode

GHOST OF EX-MAS PAST

A SPICY SECOND CHANCE NOVELLA

WINTER WANDERLUST
BOOK 3

LIZ ALDEN

GHOST OF EX-MAS PAST

Copyright © **2024 Liz Alden**

All rights reserved.

ISBN-13 (ebook): 978-1-954705-38-8

ISBN-13 (paperback): 978-1-954705-46-3

ISBN-13 (large print): 978-1-954705-53-1

Published by **Liz Alden**

No parts of this publication may be reproduced, stored in a retrieval system, or transmitted in any form or by any means, electronic, mechanical, photocopying, recording, or otherwise, without the prior written permission of the copyright owner.

This book is sold subject to the condition that it shall not, by way of trade or otherwise, be lent, resold, hired out, or otherwise circulated without the publisher's prior consent in any form of binding or cover other than that in which it is published and without a similar condition including this condition being imposed on the subsequent purchaser. Under no circumstances may any part of this book be photocopied for resale. No part of this book may be used for the purpose of training artificial intelligence systems or machine learning.

This is a work of fiction. Any similarity between the characters and situations within its pages and places or persons, living or dead, is unintentional and coincidental.

First Edition

Library of Congress Control Number: 2024920077

League City, Texas, United States of America

Proofread by Annette Szlachta

Cover Design by Qamber Designs

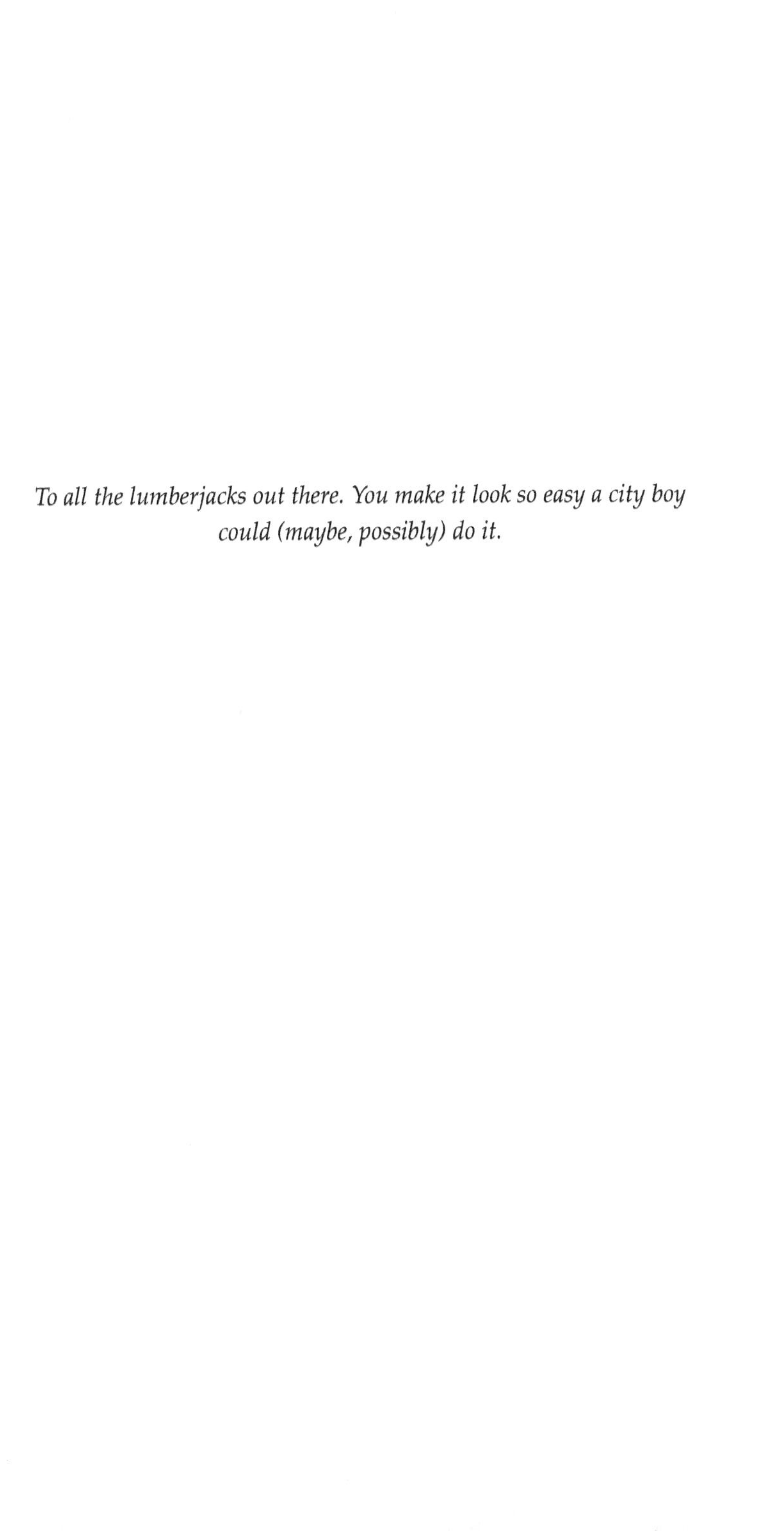

To all the lumberjacks out there. You make it look so easy a city boy could (maybe, possibly) do it.

1

BEA

I'm having the best Hallmark-induced daydream ever.

I've traded the Manhattan office I'm currently sitting in for a crystal-clear blue sky above me and trees around me. The frozen lake is perfectly smooth and the pines are snowcapped and picturesque. I'm surrounded by townsfolk and gracefully skating along until I lock eyes with a handsome, flannel-clad man skating toward me. He gives me a slow smile, and then I trip on something—a bump in the ice, maybe—and I fall, but like, in a *sexy* way, and he catches me and—

Okay, scratch that. First of all, if anyone can fall in a "sexy way," it's not me. I've never ice-skated before, not even a few blocks away at Rockefeller Center, which is packed right now since it's December. Second, I am not even sure a small town in the Catskills like Here, New York, is going to have a skating rink. Sure, Here looks cute as hell, but it's also pretty tiny—one small ski resort and a handful of restaurants and shops that make up Main Street.

Fine. Well, what if I take the flannel idea for a run with a different fantasy? In the backyard of the cabin my family is renting for the holidays I hear this loud thwacking noise. It's a lumberjack—beard and everything—chopping wood for us.

He catches sight of me, drops the axe (in a careful, safe way so he doesn't lose any toes), and sweeps me into his arms. We make out against the woodpile, my hands running underneath that flannel until—

Damn it. It's cold outside. My nips would cut glass.

Unless he's got a fire going.

Well, that wouldn't solve the problem of splinters from the log pile. I do not want rough-hewn wood anywhere near my sensitive parts, thank you very much.

What if I'm in one of Here's adorable locally owned shops and we both reach for the same . . . I don't know, snow globe? And our hands touch and there's a spark of electricity and—

"Bea? Hello? Earth to Bea!"

I blink back into focus and out of my daydream.

Sigh. Goodbye, sexy mountain man.

Instead I'm in my boss's office with him and his wife. It's not unusual for us to have a casual lunch together. Clara often brings in food for both of us and she knows the *best* restaurants.

But right now, their attention is on me and Clara is smirking.

"Sorry, did you need something?" I ask, ready to put my food down—bao buns from that Chinese place a few blocks away—and step back into my job as executive assistant.

Nash shakes his head, a small smile on his face. "No, but your phone's been buzzing nonstop."

"Shit." I snatch up my phone from the arm of the chair and check the notifications. Way to be snoozing on the job, Bea.

"Not that one," Clara corrects. "The one in your purse."

Oh. Well, that's my personal phone. I feel less bad, though my phone buzzing enough to annoy Clara—not technically my boss but close enough—isn't great either.

Don't get me wrong. I like Clara and Nash a lot. Nash is the CEO of Heartly, a social media company built on positive vibes and wholesome content, and Clara runs food tours in the city focused on immigrants and their food culture. Calling them friends wouldn't be accurate, though—this is business.

I pull my personal phone out and check the screen. Oh boy. I've got email notifications popping up like crazy.

Usually my phone is on Do Not Disturb during the workday, but I have it scheduled to be off during my break. I often leave it at my desk, like when we have meetings or a work lunch, but today, since we just got back from an off-site meeting, my phone is with me.

I open my email and scroll through the messages. It's all one long thread and in my head I form a quick "TL;DR": Dad wants to change the rules of our family secret Santa. The rest of the messages are mostly my three sisters chiming in something to the effect of *no way* and *Why? The way we do it is fun.*

Secret Santa isn't something I need to worry about right now, so I turn DND back on and tuck my phone away.

"Anything interesting?" Clara raises a dark eyebrow at me.

I shrug. "Christmas planning."

"You're going upstate, right?" Nash asks. He's in a suit, like always, this one a deep blue that complements his dark features. I know so much about Nash, not only from working for him but from all the media attention he gets. He's young, handsome, the estranged son of Arab immigrants, and he recently was handed the reins of Heartly from his former mentor and surrogate father, Clara's dad.

"Yup. In the Catskills."

Clara pops the last of her bao bun into her mouth. "Let us know how it is. Maybe we'll go there next year."

She says it sincerely, but I snort inside my head. Last year, they—Nash, Clara, and her immediate family—spent the holidays in the Alps at a gorgeous chalet. This year, they're going to Finland to watch the northern lights and visit Santa Claus Village. Nash is surprising Clara with a food tour where they'll learn how the native peoples survived winters and preserved food. Since the family includes Clara's niblings, which are all under the age of seven, it seems like there's something for everyone.

Here isn't nearly on the same level of these globe-trotters' Christmas plans, but it is a hell of a step up from Pithole, PA, where my family used to spend the holidays.

I'll take it.

Clara changes the subject. "How was your date the other night?"

"Oh my god, amazing. Thank you so much for recommending that tapas place. I ordered the croquettes and they were To. Die. For. I'm serious," I insist when she laughs. "The server had to perform CPR; it was a whole scene."

"I meant the *man*."

"Oh." I wave my hand to indicate that the man I had a date with isn't even worth discussing.

There's an epidemic of shitty dates occurring across bars, restaurants, coffee shops, pubs, diners, and yes, even the occasional hot dog stand, all the time in this city. My bad dates are nothing special.

Though this one was, in fact, pretty damn bad. I don't tell guys I'm an EA super often on the first date, but this one, a finance bro who lives in Tribeca, continued to ask me about work. The disdain on his face when I said "assistant" should have had me end the date there.

Alas, my Hallmark-fueled romantic heart valiantly tried to avoid flatlining before dessert, but after Raj picked up the check and told me we were going to my place (presumably for sex), it gave up the ghost. Sadly, it was also not the first time a date has assumed he gets to have sex with me after one date.

RIP my love life. Time of death, 8:45 p.m.

That was my twelfth date in a row where I didn't like the guy enough to even kiss him. Granted, I work too much to go out on many dates, so the last time I had a man-induced orgasm was seven months ago when I swiped right and had a one-night stand while in London for meetings.

Honestly, city men just suck. There's something about the concrete jungle, smog, and incessant press of people that makes them careless. As much as I enjoy my job, there's nothing else holding me to New York.

I know how amazing love can be. I fell in love once and got left behind for a big city and all its opportunities and wealth. Furthermore—I want a family. I'm twenty-eight now, which I know is still young, but when you do the math . . . a year to date, a year to plan the wedding, a year of married bliss, then three to four kids over eight or ten years . . .

I feel old just thinking about it. And two of my sisters are in committed relationships. My kids should have cousins their own age to play with. The clock is ticking, people!

That's why I'm going to keep my options open when I get to Here. There's a flannel-clad, outdoorsy small-town man in my future. I can feel it.

There's a ding and then an echo of a ding across the room when two phones go off with calendar notifications—mine and Nash's—and it's time for us to go to the conference room for a meeting. I check my makeup and hair—flawless and smooth. Clara waves us off, insisting she'll take care of the trash and tidy up, so Nash and I grab our things and go.

On the walk, I check my personal phone again. The most recent email is from my mom, and it says, *Bea, are you okay with that?*

I'm not sure what they've settled on, but I'll catch up on the email thread later. I'm sure whatever they decide is fine.

Yup, totally fine, Mom. See you soon.

We step into the conference room and have our meeting with the advertising team. I sit next to Nash and take notes on what he needs to accomplish until I hear a familiar name.

"Wait, what did you just say?" I ask Miles, the lead.

"Uh, how far back do you want me to go?"

"The bit about Rivrse."

"Rivrse does sensors for virtual reality technology. Their product is currently being used in the ImmUniverse headsets." Miles turns back to Nash. "We've noticed that ImmUniverse is now targeting ads on our platform based on customer data they shouldn't have access to, and we think it's coming from the Rivrse sensors. A few employees are testing out their VR headsets and looking for some data points, but it'll take a while to figure out what's actually happening. We probably need to call in legal to figure out if what ImmUniverse is doing is against our policies." He grimaces.

Nash's gaze meets mine, and he raises an eyebrow, probably wondering what my sudden interest in VR headsets is about.

My brain is still catching up and trying to reconcile what I know about Rivrse—which is, actually, not much. But I do know a lot about the CEO of Rivrse . . . he's my ex.

2

CHARLIE

With every step I take away from the meeting I just left, I give more and more serious thought to screaming *FUCK* out loud.

In the five months since I've opened an office in New York, I've seen some pretty weird things. Two weeks ago, I saw a bike messenger get hit by a taxi. He jumped up unharmed, screamed, "I am god!" and sprinted down the street, leaving his bike behind with the flummoxed cabdriver.

So, basically, New Yorkers are used to some bizarre shit.

However, the man by my side keeps me from lashing out at the universe. Arlo, who's been my mentor for almost nine years, has his hand on my shoulder and squeezes once, as if he knows how pissed off I am.

It's a short walk to my new office in Two Bridges. Arlo and I enter the building, ride the elevator, and pass the approximately twenty employees that make up the New York office of my company, Rivrse, in silence.

Finally behind the closed door of my office, I sink into my chair, face in my hands.

"Fuuuuuccccckkkkkkkk."

It's quiet. Or, at least, quieter than what I wanted to do when we left ImmUniverse.

"I know it's not ideal," Arlo says. "But it's a good sign that they haven't backed out entirely."

ImmUniverse has just decided that they need more time to do their due diligence, and we've all agreed—begrudgingly on my part—to push the sale of Rivrse to ImmUniverse back till January.

"I feel like I'm being punished for making a smart financial decision," I complain. We recently signed a deal with a Korean phone manufacturer. Over the next five years, it'll double sales of our proximity sensors. I know it was a good deal, and Arlo and I discussed it ad nauseam.

"I know," Arlo says, voice full of sympathy and patience. He's got a stake in all this too—not only has he supported many of my projects, most of which haven't gone as well, but he's brokering the sale. While he mentors former university students (like me) and sits on the board of a VC firm, most of his income is from helping start-up founders (also like me) exit their businesses. "But the contract is good. ImmUniverse will review the terms and see that too. They'll be glad that you've diversified your income in the international market."

I hope so. I'd been working on this new contract since before I had decided to sell my business.

"Okay. I just wanted this to be done before the holidays so badly."

Arlo leans forward, steepling his fingers. "I know. I could see on your face how disappointed you were. And I bet they could too. But you've got to remember that if they think you'll do anything to get the sale to go through, it doesn't matter how strong your valuation is or what comes up in due diligence. They'll offer less. And I know you don't want that."

I want both. The whole point of selling Rivrse is the money. I just bought an apartment here in the city, and I want to buy my parents a new house and let my mom quit her job.

In the boardroom of ImmUniverse, I saw part of my dream crumble.

In some Christmas that will never come to pass, I announce at dinner that I've sold Rivrse and am taking time off to pursue the next thing I want most in life—a family.

It isn't just my parents sitting at the table. It's their best friends and the couple I consider my second parents, Erik and Jody. They love me like a son, and seeing the four of them beam at me in pride would be so satisfying.

Okay, well Erik and the moms would beam. My dad would probably make an impressed grunt and slap me on the back.

And then, at this fictional dinner, there would also be Jody and Erik's four daughters—three of whom are like sisters to me.

But that fourth one . . .

That fourth sister is the one I let get away.

Bea.

I make good money now. My savings account is, by most measures, huge. I'm living in the same city as Bea for the first time since we graduated high school.

I won't ever have to worry about money the way our parents did. I won't ever have to say the words Bea said our senior year of high school when we talked about college: "I can't afford it."

My kids won't ever get shipped away to their grandmother's house while their parents fight over money troubles.

If I can close this deal, I'm set up for the next phase of my life—love and family . . . maybe even with the one I let get away.

3

———

BEA

A FEW WEEKS LATER, I ARRIVE HOME FROM THE LAST PRE-HOLIDAY workday. I kick off my shoes on a sigh and walk into the living room. My roommates, Brin and Marco, are sitting very close together on the couch and Marco closes his laptop.

Maybe they were looking at porn.

We've been living together for a few months, and with my work schedule and attempts at having a dating life, I don't know them super well, but they lived together before moving in with me. Our place is a cramped two-bedroom in Manhattan, but so far they've been great roommates. Much tidier than me.

Speaking of which, before any of us can say anything, I spin around and double back to the door, where I pick up my shoes. I don't want to be *that* roommate who leaves her shit out for other people to trip on. I carry them to my bedroom and toss them inside my messy room before closing the door and turning, hands on my hips, to face my roommates.

"What are y'all up to?" I raise an eyebrow.

"Nothing," Brin says cheerily. "How was your day?"

I eye them. Marco has a great poker face—*no, of course, your dirty dishes weren't in my way*—while Brin has absolutely zero poker face. Right now, she looks guilty as hell, which is better than being annoyed that my mess has spilled out of my room.

At work, I'm hyper organized. At home, not so much. My last roommate, Michelle, was also messy, so our apartment was not great. I'm barely home, so it didn't matter much to me, but when she moved out and I deep cleaned the kitchen before posting a listing, even I had to admit it was pretty gross.

I'm disorganized, but not dirty. Michelle was *dirty*, and in my chaos, I never noticed.

Now, though, I have these two, who keep the place spotless and share a bedroom. There are two beds, so I'm not a hundred percent sure that any shenanigans are going on, but I am one hundred percent sure that they at least have pantsfeelings for each other.

I eye them, innocence and guilt side by side on my couch, and decide that if they don't want to talk about whatever's going on between them, fine, whatever. I can pretend too.

"My day was good. The office was pretty empty and I can always get more work done when that happens." I check my watch. I left work early, but not *that* early, and I only have half an hour to pack before I plan to get on the road. Traffic is going to be a bitch, and it's already a fading winter afternoon outside, so there's no way in hell I'll be making it to Here before it's dark out, but at least I can still make it in time for dinner. I'm glad I picked up my rental car this morning.

I pull my suitcase out of the tiny hall closet and clear space for it on the floor in my room, leaving the door open.

Brin and Marco share the bigger bedroom, so together they pay more of the rent. It works out well for all of us. I make good money at Heartly, but rent in the city is bonkers expensive. Marco is a personal assistant and works for a highnet-worth asshole. We met through a networking event for young professionals, an organization Nash encourages me to take part in for my own personal development. I haven't ever considered leaving Heartly, but I got a roommate out of it; so far it's been a win.

I thought my finance bro dates were bad, but the stories Marco brings home take the cake. Anyway, he's underpaid, and Brin is a server, so they are happy to split the rent and share space.

We chat while I throw clothes into my bag—a nice outfit for dinner out, sweaters, hats, gloves . . . everything I need for a snowy getaway. Marco's boss is going away on vacation for the week, so just like me, Marco has the time off. He's wearing a suit, though, so he must have just come in from his boss's house or office or somesuch.

Throughout this whole time, neither Marco nor Brin move on the couch. They are still sitting awfully close—Brin has her legs folded beneath her, slightly overlapping Marco's knee—and it just makes me more sure that I interrupted something.

I move to the bathroom to pack my toiletries, when there's a buzz from the intercom.

"Got it!" Brin shouts. I hear her murmured voice and a staticky conversation before she appears in the doorway to the bathroom. "You're giving someone a ride?"

I sigh and hang my head. Dear god, my sister is a nightmare. "Yeah, buzz her up."

Brin shrugs and disappears.

My sister Naomi said she *might* fly into the city early to visit friends and catch a ride with me. I said that was fine, but then I never heard back from her, so I assumed she was flying into Albany with the rest of the family and just didn't tell me.

At least I don't think she did. It's entirely possible that I missed an email—or twenty—about our holiday plans.

When we were going to Pithole last year for the tenth time, there were about eleventy-billion emails coordinating plans between the ten of us. With our new location, the volume of emails has multiplied. It's *a lot* of emails with a lot of people who don't understand when to use reply all.

I'm tossing my bag of tampons and pads into my luggage —I'm expecting my period around Christmas Day, Merry Christmas to me—when Brin walks in from the front door, a looming figure behind her.

It's not my short-and-stacked sister. Instead it's someone I didn't think I'd have to see this Christmas—Charlie Dunsky, my ex and the founder of Rivrse.

"What are you doing here?" I blurt out. No, no, no. I thought I was getting a Christmas *without* Charlie. I hadn't heard anything about him coming, and I distinctly remember there was a spreadsheet with flight times and coordinating driving from the Albany airport to Here and Charlie's column had been blank. Plus, there was an email from his mom saying something about him moving . . .

Although, when was the last time I checked that spreadsheet?

Charlie blinks at me. "You're giving me a ride." It comes out like *duh*.

Oh, for fuck's sake.

"When did I say that?"

"Well, you didn't. You had offered Naomi a ride and your mom asked if you could give me a ride instead." At my glare, he shrugs. "You said yes." There's a bit of defensiveness in his voice.

My roommates crowd together on the couch again, their gazes ping-ponging between me and Charlie.

Of course, the moms have something to do with it. Hell, both of our families are as steeped in our relationship as we are. That's what happens when you date the boy next door, the one whose parents are best friends with your parents.

"Why didn't you fly into Albany?" My sisters are all flying into the Southwest hub, which means they can all fly standby since my youngest sister and her fiancé both work for the airline. Our parents—all four of them—packed into Charlie's parents' Suburban and drove.

Yes, they drove from Alabama, taking turns at the wheel to get there overnight. Charlie's mom, Susan, says it's "like a sleepover on wheels."

Something flutters across Charlie's face—guilt? Determination? Pride? After all these years apart, I can't read Charlie as well as I used to.

"I live in New York now."

"What?" I yelp.

"I feel like we should get popcorn," Brin whispers.

"Look, I've got a cab running downstairs with my luggage in it." Charlie points with his thumb over his shoulder. "Should I have it take me to the train station, or should I bring my stuff up?"

I rub my temples. Do I want to be spending close, personal time with Charlie, my first love and the man who shredded my heart when we were twenty? No, no I do not. But it's been almost a decade and to refuse now seems petty *and* like I am not over him.

Which I totally am.

"Get your stuff," I say.

4

CHARLIE

It's a two-and-a-half-hour drive from the city to Here, and I'll be spending it in the passenger side of Bea's rental car. She's trying so hard not to be mad, but I know her too well.

I genuinely thought she knew she was giving me a ride. I could have rented my own car, but my mom insisted we didn't need a fourth car. Bea's mom, Jody, added that she'd feel a lot better if she knew Bea had company on the dark trip up.

Of course, how could I say no after that? Driving at night sucks, especially in unknown places. Here is a pretty remote location, and if something happened to Bea, at least I'd be there to help.

Not that I know how to do anything handy, like change a tire.

I'm not used to New York City traffic yet. Having spent the last ten years living in the Bay Area—between Stanford, the tech incubator, and my office—I've spent most of my adult life out west. And Bea has spent most of her time living in this city.

"There's a *CROSSWALK* right there!" she shouts at someone dodging traffic to cross Amsterdam Avenue. A few

17

minutes later she honks aggressively at a Yellow Cab that forces her to slam on her brakes.

"Wow, driving in the city brings out a whole different side of you," I joke.

Good job, Charlie. The first words you've said to her in ten minutes are teasing her. Are you trying to break the ice or layer it?

"We're not in Kansas anymore, Toto," Bea mutters.

"What?"

She sighs. "I had to get used to driving in the city. My first boss treated me more like a personal assistant, so I was often moving his car. It sucked until my roommate taught me how to drive like a New Yorker."

I grab the oh-shit bar as she swerves.

"No wonder your mom wanted me to ride with you," I say under my breath.

"What?"

"Nothing."

She gives me the stink eye. It would be best to redirect her ire.

"Never saw traffic like this in Mobile. Or anywhere else. I'm sorry your boss treated you like a PA."

She shrugs. "I got a better job."

Bea and I have seen each other every year at Christmastime since our breakup. I hear about her job over unwrapped presents and big family meals. During the rest of the year, I've seen peeks of her life via social media posts and updates from our families.

Bea is gorgeous and lives in the big city. How she's still single is one of the great mysteries of the universe. I was an idiot to let her go.

Traffic is thick on the GW Bridge, and it's stop-and-go for a while. Bea doesn't say anything, just focuses on driving, while the radio plays pop music—she didn't bother to connect her phone, and I'm wondering if that's because she's too distracted by me.

Once we get on the Palisades Parkway, I pull out my laptop. My legal team sent over some new documents that I haven't had the time to read yet. PDF'd legalese is too hard on my phone, so I open up the files on the big screen and dive in.

Many people would look at a coding screen full of Python or Rust and complain about not making sense of it. I feel the same way about legal documents, but right now, they hold the key to selling Rivrse.

Dealing with my burnout was scary. It turned me into someone I didn't recognize. One day I snapped and yelled at Arlo. Thank god it was him and not one of my thirty-seven employees in the San Francisco office. But he forced me to look back and realize that nothing had been sudden—for the previous few months, I hadn't been sleeping well, and I'd been driving myself harder and harder at the expense of my body.

Of course, I didn't listen at the time because I'm a stubborn asshole, but it kept getting worse. And then it was one of the scariest moments of my life, to see everything I'd ever wanted slipping out of my hands because I couldn't focus, couldn't get out of bed.

Now I have almost the same feeling, but it's not me this time. I'm on the cusp of selling my business and every day, there seems to be more and more foot-dragging happening.

Once this deal closes, all these worries will just slough right off, like unfastening a cape that was choking me and letting it fall to the floor.

And most of all, this will prove that the greatest sacrifice of my life was worth it. I left Bea and my family behind so that they would never have to worry about money ever again. I'm so close to that success, I'm starting to dream about what my future—our future—could be like.

One possible future sits in the car next to me, humming along to a Chappell Roan song.

The eight years since Bea and I broke up have nurtured my workaholic tendencies and loneliness. I haven't been celibate, but dating has been a nightmare. Arlo says I have Bea on a pedestal, which is probably true.

It's hard to forget your first love, especially when you didn't value it like you should have.

The song ends and switches to a commercial break. Bea shifts in her seat before glancing at me. "How come I didn't know you were in the city?"

"I didn't know I was going to move until a few weeks ago. Rivrse opened an office here and I flew back and forth for a bit and then realized I needed a change in scenery. I didn't tell my parents I bought a place until last week."

Bea switches lanes to pass a slow eighteen-wheeler and goes quiet.

Arlo already lived in New York, and when Rivrse needed to open a new office, he'd suggested the city. It made sense—it put us closer to a majority of our clients and made it easier to hire a European salesperson.

I thought about reaching out to Bea. Had fantasized about the conversation, actually.

But the deal keeps getting pushed back and now that conversation would have gone something like this:

Hey, I live near you now, but I have this demanding job that was my dream but now eats away at my mental health so maybe someday when I actually get the business sold we can get together again?

The song changes, and the first strains of "Just the Way You Are" by Bruno Mars play. When I glance up from my laptop, Bea is frowning at the road ahead of us. She must feel the weight of my stare on her because her eyes dart in my direction and then down to the steering wheel.

The channel switches, and we're no longer listening to the crooning voice.

I don't take my eyes off Bea, though. She's much more

interesting than what's on my laptop screen. Her blond hair is down, her blue eyes a deep oceanic color in the fading light. One of my favorite features of Bea is the dimple on either side of her cheeks when she smiles. I have not merited a smile yet today, so the dimples stay hidden.

"Just the Way You Are" was "our song" when we were lovesick teens who thought we were going to be together forever.

Or at least, I did. I was always a goner for Bea, from the very first moment I realized that someday I might fall in love and get married. This was years before I did anything about it. Years filled with inappropriate boners and the inability to focus on anything other than her lips. Years when I was learning what things like blow jobs were and not under-standing why I would ever want to do that with anyone other than her.

In fact, I think this song was playing the first time I went down on her. Obviously, my sixteen-year-old self thought it was hella romantic, but looking back, I did not know what I was doing.

Except that I loved it.

Bea didn't enjoy it as much as I did. I don't even remember anymore if she came—she had to have, right?—but she didn't let me do it often, and maybe I wasn't as good at it as I'd thought.

Back then.

Given the chance, I'd pull this car over and wear her thighs like earmuffs.

"Stop." Bea's voice is sharp and chiding, pulling me back into the present.

I grin, and Bea ignores me. She knows exactly what I was thinking about.

Ah, well. At least I have 283 pages of legalese to get rid of this boner.

5

BEA

OF COURSE, CHARLIE WOULD PULL OUT HIS LAPTOP. HE'S THE biggest workaholic I know, and heaven forbid anything stand in his way of getting work done.

Seems like nothing's changed. Charlie's still the supersmart, super-dedicated nerd, despite growing up to be superhot.

Living next door to each other meant that I'd seen Charlie nearly every day for years. We're the same age, so it was no surprise when we were often in class together, and then we started walking to school together, playing together, studying together . . .

I knew Charlie was smarter than me from day one, when I was trying to figure out how to get my swing untangled and Charlie helped me. It was a convoluted twist for a six-year-old to manage, but Charlie could figure it out. I thought it was magic.

By the time I was fifteen, we'd grown so close. Looking back, it seemed inevitable that we'd get together. What better person to fall in love with than your best friend?

I would give my left boob to have a best friend to fall in love with now.

We had five years of being each other's firsts—first kiss, first date, first boyfriend/girlfriend, and a bunch of naughty NSFW firsts that I am *not* going to think about sitting in the car with Charlie. Even the summer he spent living with his grandma in Pithole, Pennsylvania (which, by the way, is named appropriately), wasn't enough to tear us apart.

But Charlie's education was.

By senior year, he hardly took any of the same classes I did. He was on the AP track and taking dual-credit courses at the local community college. I was a middling student who almost failed my tenth-grade science class.

I can admit my own faults, and I'm glad that at eighteen, I understood that my parents' middle-class standing meant that they couldn't afford to send four kids to college. Charlie understood it too, but he is so damn smart, he worked his ass off to get a full scholarship to Stanford.

Which left me behind in Mobile.

We're driving along the Hudson and it's full-on dark now. My grip on the steering wheel is tight, and I take a deep breath and loosen my fingers.

"Need me to take a turn driving?" Charlie asks.

"Nope."

This is why I hate the holidays. Seeing Charlie for a week every December dregs up all kinds of memories that I spend the rest of the year blissfully ignoring.

Like the memories of constantly trying to coordinate schedules between the two of us just for a chance to talk on the phone Charlie's freshman year of college, when we were trying to make the long-distance thing work.

Or the sheer frustration of not being able to catch up with bills and finding adulting to be so difficult, even though I had a full-time job as an office admin. I'd made the stupid mistake of buying a car that was too nice for me and then getting in a fender bender that ate up all of my savings when I'd almost had enough to fly out to California and see Charlie.

And now Charlie lives in the same city as I do. At least it's a huge city, and the chances that I'll run into him are slim. He might as well still live in San Francisco.

Next to me, Charlie closes his laptop and turns his face to the window. My phone tells me to exit and we pull away from the river and into the interior of the state.

I wonder what Charlie was working on. I asked Miles for an update about the sensor-data-targeting advertising issue that was brought up at the meeting, but they're still experimenting.

Would Charlie do something unethical, maybe even illegal, to get ahead? I'm not sure. Ten years ago I would have said no. But what do I really know about Charlie now?

I startle a bit when Charlie speaks. "Are you glad we aren't going to Pithole this year?"

"Yeah. Pithole was . . ." I struggle to think of the right word without offending Charlie. We always went to Pithole because that's where his grandma had lived. It was a dying town, but when his grandma was alive, the Dunskys had, every December 22, packed up their son and Christmas presents and drove to Pithole to spend Christmas with his grandma.

When she died during our junior year of high school, the Dunskys invited my family to join them.

"It was a pit hole; you can say it."

I wince, though *pit hole* is a much nicer word than I would use. In fact, it's a much nicer word than what I used back then. My sisters and I, being catty teenagers who already thought anything to do with our family was uncool, had verbally roasted the place when we first saw it until, furious, my dad had dragged us aside and told us that ungrateful girls get their Christmas presents donated to charity.

"It was a pit hole," I allow, "but it was our pit hole."

"True. I guess we'll have to find a new pit hole." The way he says it is a little cheeky, and I bite my tongue before a that's-what-she-said joke slips out. "Have you been upstate before?"

Psht. With my job, I travel for work, and not the other way around. Nash and I travel the world for our work, so there's no way I have time to travel for fun. I barely have time to date. "No."

"Me neither."

There's a moment of quiet while the streetlights flash past us. I don't want to admit it, but I am excited to visit Here. There was very little to enjoy about Pithole and nothing to do outside the house (except join my mom on her walking expeditions or my dad on his five-times-a-day grocery store visits), and one week is plenty of time to build alliances and backstab over several Monopoly games, so we often got a serious case of cabin fever.

This year, there's shopping, dining, skiing—no ice-skating, so I'll have to rely on Tinder to help me discover a small-town romance instead—and the house we are renting is a significant upgrade from the cabin we would stay at in Pithole.

All that being said, our parents love the trips up north for the winter.

"I wonder why we're not going back," I muse.

Charlie turns to me, resting an elbow on the car door. "It might have been because the infamous Marinara Stain of 2022 was still present on the couch in 2023. I thought your mom was going to give herself a heart attack while disinfecting the house."

I smile. She'd bought, like, eight different bottles of cleaning supplies and said that if a rental place is choosing to flip the couch cushions over instead of cleaning them, then who knows what else they skimp on. "My mom? Your dad was the one who went on and on about the fact that they charged us for damages and clearly they'd taken the money and run."

There's a flash of white teeth as Charlie smiles too. "He

hates wasting money. Remember that one year after the Shop-Rite in Pithole had closed and Dad had wanted to stop at the Giant on the way in so that he could save gas?"

"Oh my god, yes. I couldn't believe your mom put her foot down." Charlie's mom, Susan, is a pretty carefree, go-with-the-flow lady. But after an overnight drive, the last thing any of us wanted to do was shop for a week's worth of food for nine people. "It makes it even more bizarre that we're renting such a nice place in Here. It's such an upgrade. I'm surprised our parents wanted to spend the money."

There's a beat of silence and I mentally kick myself. Long ago, our parents agreed to split the rental costs per person so the Dunskys aren't footing a disproportionate bill. Money has always been a sore spot for the Dunskys, and I shouldn't judge how they want to spend it. I don't know how to recover from my faux pas, so I say nothing.

Charlie turns his face away from me and looks out the window again.

6

CHARLIE

THIS IS WHAT I'M UP AGAINST. BEA AND I HAVE SO MANY minefields to navigate, it makes it hard to see a path forward.

I can't comment on paying for the cabin in Here. I'm proud, but I don't think it'll go over well and, besides, it would open a can of worms, and there's the NDA to think of.

I wish, for the thousandth time, that I'd understood at age twenty that what Bea and I had was irreplaceable. That I'd worked harder, saved more money, and kept Bea in my life. Would we be navigating this together?

We drive through a few small towns, the terrain getting hillier as the miles go by. In my senior year of college, I allowed myself *one* splurge—a friend's family had a house in Lake Tahoe. I spent a week there learning to ski, and I know that the Catskills, while beautiful, offer a better beginner-skier experience than skiing out west. Which is good, since Bea doesn't know how to ski.

Finally, we make it to Here. We have to drive through the town to get to the cabin, which is closer to the ski resort. Bea slows the car and we both peer out the windshield at the glowing Christmas decorations.

Bea gasps when she sees a giant Christmas tree in the town center, and something in me swells.

This year could be different.

A new leaf.

"Wow," she says, and I don't think she's talking to me, but I agree anyway. The tree is enormous, and I'm not sure what magic exists in Here, New York, but the lights are moving along the tree, dancing and twinkling while they wind their way up.

There's a honk and Bea lets out a small "whoops" before jolting the car back into motion. She glances in the rearview mirror, watching the tree fade away behind us.

Outside town, the car starts up a steady incline. We drive past the ski resort, which has its own Christmas tree out front, but this one looks to be planted. It doesn't have magical dancing lights but big, shiny baubles adorn it and there's a star on top.

The next turn is a small road. There are a few houses, but there's enough space between them that the glow from one home doesn't touch the other. Then, one last turn, and Bea gasps again.

I recognize the rental I booked. The house is glorious. Each forward-facing window has an electric candle in it and the double front door boasts two wreaths twined with gold ribbon and holly sprigs. White lights line the roof, a wire Santa and his sleigh perch next to a chimney, and the Christmas tree glows through the front picture window. People move around inside, reminding me of that scene in *Home Alone* where Macaulay Culkin creates a cardboard-only holiday party, but here all the people are real.

And when our headlights pan across the window, it reveals six faces pressed up against the glass.

We barely come to a stop beside my parents' old Suburban when the door flies open.

"Watch the wreath!" someone shouts. One of Bea's sisters.

"Watch it do what?" That's Bea's dad.

My mom cackles, ever the dutiful audience member for Erik's dad jokes.

The crowd flows on either side of the car, and someone opens my door for me. I step out and am immediately wrapped in an incense-scented hug.

My mom.

She hugs me for a good thirty seconds and then rears back. "Your vibes are murky right now."

"Vibes?" I raise an eyebrow.

She ignores me. "Desperation. And you've been working too hard."

"That's not new." The interjecting voice is Bea's sister Kayla. Once my mom gives her enough room, Kayla wraps her arms around my waist and squeezes too tight.

I blow a raspberry in her ear and she laughs. I have to bend down slightly to deliver it, as Kayla is the shortest of the Cummings girls. She squeezes again and I oblige with another fake fart.

I've always considered Kayla, Naomi, and Yvette to be my sisters. But never did I once think of Bea that way.

I work my way through eight more hugs with seven more people—Mom comes back in for another hug—before the crowd moves inside. Dad, Erik, and Lance, Yvette's fiancé, are already handling our luggage, so I grab my laptop bag from the front seat and make my way inside.

The living room, the room with the tree we could see from the driveway, shows signs of a party—wineglasses on all surfaces, one of those pre-made cheese-and-veggie party platters on the table, and music playing from hidden speakers. One of Bea's sisters is giving her a tour, and their dad hooks my elbow and starts our own tour.

"From the living room, you can go right into the kitchen

from the butler's pantry." Erik gestures. "Would you believe there are zero butlers stocked in here? I told Jody we should have swung by Costco on our way up to grab a pack of twelve."

Behind me, Naomi groans.

The kitchen's huge, and we stall out there. Bea's tour took the other route into the kitchen, and when she finally gets a good look at her dad, Bea laughs. "Dad, what the hell is up with your hair?"

Erik threads his fingers on either side of his head and pulls his hair away from his scalp. "Do you like it?" When he lets go, his brown wavy hair falls to brush against his shoulders.

"That's like, Matthew McConaughey hair."

"All right, all right, all right."

"Don't give him bongos, for the love of god," Naomi shouts.

"You know why he keeps getting invited to Naughty By Nature concerts?"

This time, the entire room groans—except my mom, predictably.

"Because he's Matthew Ma-conna-heyyyy, ho, hey, ho!"

There's a chorus of "Daaaaddddd!"

The tour of the house goes like that for the next hour. Mom assures me she's saged the house and she'll put the furniture back before she leaves, but "isn't the feng shui of the room *so much better*?" In the sunroom, Jody has set up her yoga mat and tells us she's gotten into yoga because it keeps her "hips flexible."

"She has to keep up with her hot young husband," Erik jokes, planting a smacking kiss on Jody, who's six years older than him.

"Ew," Naomi says.

"Now, honey," my mom starts, and I know where this is

going. "Your mother is a vibrant woman and has needs. There's nothing gross about her sexuality."

"Moving on," my dad says, saving us from more sex conversations by herding us out of the room to finish the downstairs tour. Each space is decorated for Christmas, from a Nativity scene to miniature trees with tiny ornaments to real garland twined around the banister on the stairs.

Everyone else has been here for hours already, but they still feel the need to show us around and provide their own commentary. After a long car ride of mostly silence with Bea, it's a welcome cacophony that continues through dinner, meatloaf made by Yvette and Lance.

(Erik tells us *meatloaf* is the best safe word to use, and Naomi tells him she's heard that joke before. Erik shrugs and says, "What, do I have to have original content?" and then we have to explain to my dad what a safe word is.)

Finally, when everyone's done eating, Jody says, "It's time to draw for the secret Santa!"

I groan, because this is going to take ages.

Jody gets up to gather supplies, and my dad pulls a pen out of his shirt pocket.

Bea clears her throat. "So, uh, remind me what the new rules are again?"

Everyone stills for about two seconds, glancing at each other until they burst out laughing.

"The rules haven't *changed*," Jasper, Kayla's husband, says.

"There was a whole email thread," Bea insists.

"Yes, well, your father got the harebrained idea that we should do white elephant gifts instead—"

"I found the perfect gag gift," Erik interrupts.

"—but we unanimously vetoed him because we're all adults and the last thing we need is people fighting over gifts that are just going to go into the trash in a month or two."

"Exactly right," Mom agrees.

Our secret Santa rules are simple: we draw names the first night together, and then we have to buy the present from somewhere local for less than twenty dollars. In Pithole, this was often a favorite snack from the supermarket or miscellaneous crap from the fly-fishing store (completely negating the idea that our secret Santa gifts have never been wasteful and each recipient cherished their gift, but I digress). This year, we're excited to have actual gift shops to shop in, and that was the third biggest reason not to change the rules—behind tradition and no one wanting to feel bad for stealing the better gifts.

"I still have the white elephant gift from my office exchange two years ago." Erik turns to the rest of the table and brags, "It's a reindeer that poops candy."

"I'm sure someone will get you something just as tacky as a pooping reindeer," Jody assures him, returning to the room with paper and a glass bowl.

Erik sighs good-naturedly with a lopsided grin.

"So," Jasper reiterates. "No changes."

"God, Bea, read your emails," Kayla gripes.

Bea glares at her sister. "I read my emails—"

"Clearly."

"—I have a *job*."

"Girls." Jody uses her no-nonsense tone and Bea and Kayla snap their jaws shut. Bea's sisters love to razz her about my big-city job.

"Okay, now, everyone write your name on a paper, fold it up, and throw it in the bowl," Jody explains, as if we haven't been doing this for the past decade.

She distributes pens and paper and soon the bowl is full of wadded-up paper balls. Jody produces a twelve-sided die and rolls it, reading six from the ivory face, and counts clockwise from her left till she points at Lance. He draws a name, reads it, and stuffs it in his jeans pocket.

The next roll is eleven, and Jody starts the count from the

seat to Lance's left, until she lands on Bea. And so on, until Jody's finger points at me.

I close my eyes and reach into the bowl, swirling around the rustling balls until it feels right.

I pluck the paper out and read the name while Jody moves on.

Bea.

7

CHARLIE

Somehow through the years I've managed not to draw her in the secret Santa game, so the last gift I gave Bea was our final Christmas as a couple, eight years ago.

It was a disaster. Worst holiday ever, and only partly because I didn't come home for Christmas for the first time.

At Stanford, I still needed money for all the small expenses my scholarship didn't cover. I worked a retail job, and the manager had offered me additional hours during their busiest time of year. My parents had been disappointed but understood—Bea was a different story. I told her that if I worked over the Christmas break, the wages, bonuses, and tips would carry me through the summer.

"So you'll be home this summer?" Bea had asked.

"For a few weeks," I said.

She'd gone silent. Dangerously silent. And then we'd argued about it for hours.

"I miss you. Come home. We can live together and save more money." This was her constant position, that everything would be better if I abandoned the opportunity that I'd worked for, the money that was handed to me, and came home.

"And go where? Alabama doesn't have any schools that compare to Stanford. And I've already got a mentor and he's helping me choose a summer internship. This was always my plan."

"But I never see you. We don't even talk anymore. I'm building this life here and you're building one there and how will they ever be the same?"

"I don't know!"

Even as angry as we were, we stayed together for a few more weeks. I thought sending the necklace would help, that it would remind her of how much I loved her every time she wore it.

Instead it was the final nail in the coffin. Bea and I barely wished each other a Merry Christmas when Mom passed the phone around, and her whispered "Thank you" after opening my present was sad.

The next week, we broke up.

You know what they say about long-distance relationships: they never work.

I tuck the paper into my pocket without looking at Bea. After the names are all drawn, the party moves to the kitchen and resumes while Bea and her sisters jockey over doing the dishes (because whoever doesn't clean up tonight has to clean up after Jasper tomorrow night; he'll be cooking dinner *and* baking up a storm) while the rest of us help ourselves to the store-bought sugar cookies.

"Not as good as yours," I say, and Jasper raises his cookie to me in a salute.

I end up next to my dad. He's shorter than me, shaved bald and with a neatly trimmed goatee. Working in the Frito-Lay factory gave him a stocky build and for most of my life, I remember him as a fit man, stripping off his back brace when he got home from work. Now he's still exercising, but he has the paunch of a man whose body is succumbing to age.

"Hey, Dad."

His lips tip up in what passes for a smile. He's a quiet man, the opposite of Erik. "How's your new place?"

"Really nice. I have a great view." My new condo in the city is a block off Central Park, and I can see patches of the green expanse if I angle my head just right. I lower my tone and step closer to my dad so no one else can hear. "When are you going to let me improve your view?"

He grunts and crosses his arms. Mom and Dad still live in the same house we moved to when I was sixteen and Dad got laid off. When we had to move away from the Cummingses. "There's nothing wrong with our house."

I bite my tongue on criticizing it. It's cluttered, but with my mom that's par for the course. She collects a lot of shit and the yard in front of the run-down two-bedroom house is full of tchotchkes, and the roof over the tiny front porch sags under all of Mom's wind chimes.

"Mom could quit working if you let me buy you a house. They're so cheap in Mobile, I can buy you one back in Morning Dale." That's the neighborhood where we used to live next door to Bea's family—the one they still live in.

Dad's gaze meets mine. "That argument would hold more weight if you actually got your mother on board first."

Okay, so Mom loves waitressing at the diner. She likes chatting with the regulars and thinks she makes good money in tips. The reality is that she makes a pittance and she's fifty-eight; she can't stay on her feet forever.

"Besides," Dad says, his voice sharpening. "Don't think I haven't noticed you went way over budget on this house."

"I am perfectly on budget on the house."

Dad shakes his head. "The lift passes, the decorations, the food delivery," he fumes. "We had an agreement."

"Our agreement was that I would limit what I spent on the house. I did."

He rolls his eyes. "If you think I'm going to let that loophole slide, you've got another think comin', son."

"Fine," I bite out. "Believe what you want. I—" I shut down my retort when I see Jasper breaking away from the rest of the group and approaching us. When he gets here, he crosses his arms and hunches over, brows scrunched down. "What are we talking about? Global warming? Mass extinction? The systematic degradation of individual rights?"

I glance down at myself. Just like my dad, I have my arms crossed and my shoulders curved in. Simultaneously, Dad and I straighten and drop our arms.

Jasper grins and does the same. He's taller than me, with dark skin from his Jamaican parents and a close-trimmed fade and a beard.

"How's life back in Tampa?" I ask, diverting the conversation away from anything that will get our hackles up again.

"Good. Kayla is gearing up for the slew of newly engaged brides who need her makeup artistry for their photoshoots. All the holiday proposals, you know."

"Romantic," Dad says gruffly.

"I'm surprised you could get away from the restaurant," I comment. Jasper didn't join us last year because restaurants are so busy over the holidays.

"I quit," he says.

It's flippant, which is so like him, but my jaw drops and my eyebrows come together. "What are you going to do?"

"After the holidays, I'll look for a new job. Something with better hours." Now it's his turn to cross his arms, and he pops his hip against the counter where we're standing.

At least, until his wife calls across the room. "Babe," Kayla says, widening her eyes and looking at my dad.

"Oh, right." Jasper straightens. "I need to run to the store. Can I get your keys, or do you mind moving your car for me?"

"What do you need from the store?" Dad asks. "I can get it for you."

My dad loves to run to the store. And my mom is pretty

forgetful, so my parents' day-to-day life is my mom forgetting to buy things at the store and my dad running to get them for her.

"Nothing," Jasper says quickly. Too quickly. "Just, you know . . . women's stuff."

Dad levels him with a gaze. He may not have had a daughter himself, but he's been around the Cummings family enough. "I've bought pads and tampons for every woman in this house before. What kind?"

Jasper sighs, eyes rolling to the ceiling. "It's not tampons. Can you just move your car so I can get the rental out?"

"Nope." My dad has a really dry sense of humor when he wants to and razzing Jasper is his favorite time to whip it out.

"Shit." Jasper rubs his eyebrows. "Fine, it's . . . I forgot to get decaf coffee."

My gaze immediately goes to Kayla, and Dad turns enough that I know he's looking at her too. She's sitting with her mom and Bea, laughing and drinking a clear, carbonated beverage. Not wine, like everyone else.

Kayla's on the softer side, and she's wearing jeans and a blouse, so I can't tell if she's showing.

When I look back at Jasper, he's pinching the bridge of his nose.

"Dude," I whisper out the side of my mouth. "You could have just said decaf in the first place without being all sus about it, and we probably wouldn't have said anything." I clear my throat and return to normal volume. "Well, maybe not. Drinking decaf is weird. Nevertheless, now I'm like ninety-five percent sure I'm going to be an uncle."

"Don't." He sighs again. "We're still in the first trimester." He runs a hand down his face. "Kayla's going to kill me."

My dad's face splits into the biggest grin. A heart-achingly wide grin so large I can count his fillings. He leans over and clasps Jasper on the shoulder before digging the car keys out of his pocket. "Better run before she catches you. We won't say a word."

Jasper beats a hasty retreat and my dad schools his face. We lean against the counter behind us, side by side.

"It's starting," Dad marvels. "The next generation."

I look at Bea. She's drinking white wine, holding the stem in one hand, elbow propped up on the other hand banded under her breasts. Her dimples are out in full force, her golden hair tumbling down in waves to brush the carmine sweater she wears.

She looks like Christmas magic.

If we'd stayed together, maybe we would have had the first kid. Years ago, we might have announced at Christmas that Bea was pregnant. There would, by now, be a toddler to buy gifts for and four grandparents who would fight over babysitting.

The image is so thick in my head I have to blink it away, this vision of another Christmas that will never come to pass.

The first grandchild will be someone else's.

8

BEA

It's late by the time I go upstairs. I lightly run my hands over the garland wrapped on the banister as I make my way up. I'm glad that my parents can afford it—they split the rental with the Dunskys, even though my sisters and I, all with full-time jobs now, offered to chip in. But my parents, who smartly planned for continuing education for their four daughters, only needed to pay for various trade schools—nursing for Naomi, cosmetology for Kayla, and flight attendant school for Yvette. They seem to be comfortable enough in their finances and in good enough health that retirement isn't even on the table yet.

Personally, I think they're waiting to see which of us gives them grandkids first.

There are three doors open at the end of the hall, one of which must be mine. I push the left one open slightly only to come barreling into Charlie.

"Oh, sorry," I say when we both jump. He's carrying clothes and a small canvas bag.

"It's okay." He gestures across the hall. "I'm going to shower and get ready for bed, unless you need the bathroom."

"We're sharing?"

His mouth quirks. "Four couples and three singles. We're lucky we're not sharing a room."

"Good point. Just let me know when you're done."

He nods and I carry on to the last door. I push it open and discover two bunk beds, one on either side of the room, with kiddie decor. The sheets are bright primary colors and there's an under-the-sea theme. My luggage is on the left and someone else's—I assume Naomi's—is on the right-hand side. Hers spills open, the lower bed is rumpled, and there's a bra dangling off one of the wooden posts.

Naomi's still downstairs, so I have the space to myself. Finding a house with six bedrooms is a miracle. I, once again, didn't pay much attention to the logistics.

Speaking of which, I pull out my phone and scroll search my mom's email address. There are dozens of threads with subjects such as *WHO WANTS TO GO TUBING!!* and *Meal Plan, V5.*

I open the one that says *Room Assignments*. There's a spreadsheet with columns for bedroom number, bathrooms, and occupants. The middle says things like *en-suite, jack and jill,* and *hallway* while the last column is our names bundled up.

Charlie is right. We're lucky the single people aren't all shuffled together. I take a minute to decide if I'd rather have the queen bed Charlie has, even if I have to share it with my sister. No, bunk beds are better.

In Pithole, we had a big basement with a pull-out couch and air mattresses. Last year, Kayla and Yvette slept on the pull-out while Naomi, Charlie, and I were on air mattresses on the floor.

Yes, this is much better.

And I get along well with Naomi. Maybe Kayla and I were too similar—we were both competitively into makeup and boys—but Naomi was always more of a tomboy. And while she's never called herself aromantic or asexual, she's also never mentioned the slightest interest in anyone either, preferring to call herself "committedly single."

I'm jealous of her life, still, but in a different way. Naomi loves her job as a nurse and keeps her social life in Baltimore packed. She runs with a local running club, often sending our group chat pictures of sunrise over the harbor viewed from the promenade.

I click out of the spreadsheet and spend a few minutes scrolling through the rest of the results. Searching *Charlie ride* pulls up the gift exchange thread. I read, looking more closely at the emails.

One from my mom, at the bottom, has a PS: *Charlie is coming up from the city too. I know you offered a ride to Naomi, but can you give him a ride instead?* When I didn't answer in a few hours, that's when Mom sent the follow-up asking if I was okay with the change in plans.

And I'd said yes. Damn it.

I exit out and see that I have unread text messages. I click the notice.

> BRIN
>
> How's your family? And the house? Is it absolutely gorgeous up there?
>
> You wouldn't believe the assignment Marco's boss gave him. I'm sure you're busy with your family, but I can't wait to tell you all about it when you get home!

I text her back, telling her the house is just as gorgeous as I'd hoped. She doesn't respond—she's probably at work.

Across the hall, the bathroom door creaks open and Charlie slips out. "Bathroom's all yours," he says with a head tilt. His hair is damp and pushed back and his white shirt has transparent spots where drops of water fell onto it.

"Thanks," I say, looking away from the drips and gathering my toiletries.

When I get out of the shower, Naomi's in our room, lying on her bed and scrolling on her phone.

"My turn." She pops up and gathers the stack of clothes at her feet.

I put my dirty clothes in the corner and duck my head to get into bed. A muffled voice comes from the other side of the wall—Charlie. I wonder who he's talking to so late at night. A girlfriend?

It doesn't matter. I'm exhausted, and I curl up in bed and fall asleep to the soft rise and fall of his muffled voice.

———

IN THE MORNING, I WAKE UP WHILE IT'S STILL DARK OUT. Naomi's bed is empty, so I slip out of our room and tiptoe downstairs. The living room is also empty, but I hear voices and follow them to a door that opens to a staircase heading down to the basement.

Naomi and Kayla are on either corner of the couch, feet up between them, and looking at me when I come to the bottom of the stairs.

"Good morning," Naomi says cheerily. As a nurse, she's used to weird hours, and I'm used to her obnoxious good mood first thing in the morning. Kayla's another story. She's not a morning person, and she looks worse for the wear today. Her long blond hair is overdue for a coloring and she has circles under her eyes.

They both move their feet, making room for me to sit between them.

"What are you doing awake?" I ask Kayla. My sister's always been a little curvy, but I think she's lost weight, and with the tiredness evident on her face, I wonder if I should be concerned.

"Having trouble sleeping," she says on a sigh.

I give her a look. "Not stomach issues, right?"

She waves my concern away. "It's not the food."

"Jasper's not up?" I ask.

"He sleeps like the dead." She says it with that soft fondness she always gets when talking about her husband.

Okay, I'm jealous. I'm the oldest sister and the only thing I've really accomplished in my life is my job. My dating life sucks. But also, I barely have any friendships, and the ones I have are sparse and transactional. The people I see the most, the ones I enjoy spending time with—Brin, Marco, Clara, Nash—are fiscally tied to me.

If I moved jobs, I would lose Clara and Nash. If my roommates moved out, would I ever see them again?

Unlikely. My first roommates were when I was living in Mobile, dating Charlie. I wasn't a lot of fun back then—no hookups or wild drunken nights, which my roommates were constantly doing. I'd already lost most of my friends from high school when they went off to college. Then I broke up with Charlie and my roommates told me I was "a bummer." Moving to New York meant I lost all my friends again—I never connected with anyone. It's just not worth the effort.

This jealousy and sadness over the fact that my three sisters are now happy in their personal lives have to stop. It used to be easier, sitting on the couch with my sisters swiping through Tinder together (or in Naomi's case, providing commentary). Now, though, Kayla has her husband and Yvette has her fiancé and my love life is even more miserable than my social life.

"This basement is a big upgrade from the one in Pithole," Kayla says.

There was a basement in the house in Pithole, but this one is actually finished instead of a hodgepodge of conveniences crammed in to make it livable. This one has a big TV, a couch, and some exercise equipment.

She nudges me. "Remember watching *Elf* down there?"

I laugh, knowing exactly what time she's talking about. "When you said you had a crush on Zooey Deschanel?" I'd looked at Kayla and said, "You do?" and she said, "You don't?" and six months later Kayla announced she was bisexual.

"Ah, my queer little heart still goes pitter-patter every time I look at her."

Naomi stretches. "We'll have to watch it. After we watch the best Christmas movie of all time."

Kayla and I look at each other and roll our eyes. "*Die Hard,*" we say together.

My sisters bicker over the order of Christmas movies, but my mind wanders off to memories of the basement at the old Pithole house.

When we were sixteen, Charlie and I had somehow ended up with the entire house to ourselves for a few hours, and we were still in that phase when we were horny teenagers kissing *a lot* but too nervous to go further. Or at least, I thought that's where we'd been. But we were in the basement getting hot and heavy while making out on the couch (folded up for the day so we could watch movies on the old TV down there) when Charlie had gotten down on his knees in front of me.

It was . . . clumsy. And sweet and earnest . . . and also not super productive at all. But it was the first time for both of us and something we definitely got into—both giving and receiving—once we got back home.

"Do you think Charlie has thoughts about it?" Kayla asks, nudging me out of my memories.

"What? Probably not. Why? Wait, what?"

Naomi snickers.

"Christmas movies," Kayla says. "What did you think we were talking about?"

9

BEA

WHEN MY SISTERS AND I COME UPSTAIRS, MY MOM IS IN THE kitchen, making herself tea. Mom is tall, like Yvette, and has closely cropped white hair and glasses. Instead of a chain or some such, Mom's glasses have a no-nonsense paracord strap, which currently allows her glasses to rest on her boobs.

"There you all are," she says, putting her hands on her hips. "Who wants to go for a walk with me?"

Behind her, Naomi closes the fridge door quickly and gestures wildly at me, complete with a hand slicing across her throat, *No.*

Huh, that's weird.

Kayla says she's going to go back to bed, and Mom fusses over her for a minute, which lets me weigh my options. I work out almost every day in the city since Heartly has a great fitness center in the building. And while I would love to be completely lazy this week, I know I'll feel better if I get out and move, even if it's just a walk around the block with my mother.

"I'll go," I say, and Naomi rolls her eyes.

Mom lights up. "Wonderful. Give me fifteen minutes to finish my tea and we'll go."

I need to change out of my pajamas so I trudge up the stairs with Naomi at my heels. "What was that about?" I whisper.

"Oh you are in for it," she says, almost cackling. "Mom isn't just walking. She's power walking. She's going to leave your ass in the dust."

That's fine, I can power walk. I run five miles on the treadmill frequently.

My sister leaves me to my own folly and I dig into my luggage to find my sneakers and some yoga pants, when something glittery spills out onto the carpet.

It's a necklace, with a silver box chain that's smooth on my fingers when I pick it up and a pendant that's elegant and simple, a small round-cut diamond. It's not a great-quality stone, but I like the simplicity of it.

I've hardly ever worn it because Charlie gave it to me. It was the last present I got from him, a Christmas gift just weeks before we broke up.

Since Charlie wasn't going to be here this year, I thought it would be good to pack. My family probably doesn't remember this necklace, and it's the kind of jewelry I love—it goes with everything. It's not too extravagant but also not costume jewelry.

For now, though, I pick the jewelry up and set it back in my luggage. Now that Charlie's here, I'm not sure I'll be able to wear it.

An hour later I'm huffing and puffing my way back up the hill toward the house. Mom's ahead of me, arms pumping in perfect rhythm with her feet as her hips and shoulders swivel.

She's looped back a few times, shouting instructions at me as if I *want* to learn how to power walk. "Keep your shoulders back!" and "Really feel it in your pelvis!"

Mom's pace is in this weird middle ground where my run is too fast and my walk is too slow, so one of us is always struggling to keep up with the other. I don't have the heart to tell Mom that I'd rather run ahead or fall behind, so I give it one last attempt and make it up to the house.

Mom, who has literally power walked in circles at the top, high-fives me. "Good job, honey."

"Thanks, Mom. Do I get breakfast now?"

Indeed I do. Yvette and Lance are in charge of food this morning, and there's yogurt and granola fixings out on the counter. Everyone's downstairs in various stages of breakfast, including Charlie, whose hair Mom ruffles as she passes.

It gives me a pang in my chest. Charlie's sitting next to my dad and they're engaged in deep conversation about 401(k)s, I think?

Mom and Dad always treated Charlie like one of their own and when we broke up, it hurt them too. Susan and Gary had been their best friends ever since they'd moved in next door to us in Mobile. They'd watched each other's kids, swapped parenting advice, and, when we were old enough to take care of ourselves, went on double dates.

The first October after Charlie and I had broken up, my parents had come to me asking if I wanted to do something different for Christmas. It meant so much to me that they would offer, but at that point I had just moved to New York and had enough change in my life. While it was occasionally awkward, I look back now and can see that all four parents had run interference, distracting us with different activities just to make it through the holidays without a meltdown. And it had worked.

I don't enjoy being around Charlie, but I do it for my parents.

"Morning, Lance," I say, plopping down next to him at the dining room table.

He gives me a small smile. "Good morning." Lance and

Yvette met during their flight attendant training and after a year of commuting to see each other, Lance moved to Chicago to live with her and proposed in June. I like Lance—he's quiet but steady, and tolerates Yvette's pessimism with a grace that I can't manage most of the time, which is what probably makes him a good flight attendant too.

We chat—one-sidedly, but still—over our breakfast until Dad clinks his empty coffee mug with a spoon to get everyone's attention. "All right, team. As much as I love a lazy morning"—I check my watch; it's ten thirty already—"this to-do list isn't going to tackle itself." Dad holds up a stack of notebook papers with Mom's small, tidy writing on it. "Now, who wants to pick up the food?"

We split up tasks and divide and conquer. I spend the whole day making trips to the grocery store with my mom and Gary. Jasper joins us for the first one but then we leave him at the rental to bake cookies and banana bread, his wife as his assistant, while we make a second run. Then we have to do a third run because my spoiled-chef brother-in-law tells us we bought the wrong type of flour and not enough butter, and we comply because somehow in the two years that Jasper has been in our family, his pain au chocolat has become a tradition and it won't be the holidays without it.

Honestly, I'd forgotten how exhausting it is to haul groceries. In the city, I live two blocks away from a market and *if* I need groceries, I pick them up on my way home from work. More often than not, I order out or Brin brings home food from work. I also can't find the yogurt I like or the coconut sugar I normally put in my coffee.

Moving to a small town would take some acclimating. Who knew the city was spoiling me?

On one of the trips to the store I get from Brin.

BRIN

You won't believe the week we've been
having. We'll tell you all about it when you
get home. Hope you're enjoying the time with
your family.

XOXO

Brin and Marco

PS: I may have gotten too much into the
holiday spirit and kissed Marco. Argh! What
was I thinking?

BEA

I am having a great time. Enjoy your days off
and I'll see you soon.

PS. Wait. Am I supposed to be surprised that
you kissed him, or surprised that you haven't
been secretly banging this whole time?

She reacts with a surprised face, but nothing else, so I put my phone back in my purse. I've always thought there was something there between them, though when they moved in, they were adamant that there wasn't.

I wonder who made the first move, and what, in all the time they've lived together, what's changed now?

I don't see Charlie all day, and when Jasper banishes me and my sisters from the kitchen so he can make fried chicken in peace, we watch *Elf* in the basement. There are new decorations in the house, though; paper snowflakes that hang from the tops of the windows and a yule altar in the living room next to the fireplace, which all have the distinct stamp of Susan on them, with Charlie's help, probably.

At dinner, Charlie and I sit at opposite ends of the table. There's not a lot of talking because Jasper makes his fried chicken with buttermilk and Cajun seasoning and it's become one of our family's favorite dishes.

Afterward, though, while we're sitting around finishing our wine and barely making a dent in the cheesecake we bought at the store, Yvette disappears from the table and returns with a handful of envelopes in her hand, plus four gift bags, one black and three purple. She stands next to Lance and clears her throat. He rises and puts his arm around her waist.

"So," Yvette begins, a huge grin on her face. "We've picked a date."

My dad whoops and the rest of us laugh. Yvette passes out the envelopes. "We know it's soon," she says. "But no one had any conflicts when I asked about your schedules so . . ."

She hands me an envelope that says:

Beatrice Cummings and Guest

I hold back a snort. And who, exactly, would I be bringing?

I tear open the envelope and read the card.

Susan gasps. "Oh, it's at Magnolia Meadows! I love that place."

That's a small farm outside Mobile. I quickly scan the card. April 27, a Sunday wedding. Four months away.

"There's one other thing," my sister continues, and then she nudges her fiancé, who blushes, and hands him the black gift bag.

Lance walks around the table and sets it in front of Jasper. Jasper's eyes widen and he looks at the bag in confusion.

"Open it," Lance says.

Jasper dives in, pulling out tissue and a black box, which he sets on the table and opens. His eyes dart back and forth, reading, and then they widen even further. "What?" He jumps up from the table. "Really?"

Lance laughs and nods, and Jasper wraps him in a big

hug, lifting him off the floor and swinging him around. Mom leans over to look in the box and coos. She lifts it to show the rest of us: there's a flask, a bow tie, and cuff links, with a card that says, *Will you be my groomsman?*

Lance's feet are back on the floor now, though he and Jasper are still hugging, but now it's the back-slapping, quietly happy kind, instead of Jasper's unbridled exuberance.

"So, now that the cat's out of the *bag*," Yvette jokes, and places the three remaining bags in front of me, Naomi, and Kayla. Inside are more flasks, earrings, and a set of crystal hairpins with the card.

There's more squealing and smiles and laughter. The four of us hug, and I catch Susan wiping her eyes and Mom and Dad hugging.

Kayla peppers Yvette with wedding-related questions, and after a few minutes, we start to clear the table. I go back for another load of dishes and I catch sight of Charlie's invitation, still in front of his chair. He *also* gets a guest.

Something tugs at me uncomfortably. Charlie had RSVP'd to Kayla and Jasper's wedding last year, but then he'd had to back out at the last minute. I think he'd been ill.

I don't talk to Charlie at all after dinner and don't even see him go to bed. Which is fine by me, but when I get woken up the next morning, it's not by Naomi's alarm. Her bed is empty, and my phone says it's 7:38.

It's a rhythmic buzzing through the wall.

At first I think, *Ew, one of my sisters is using a vibrator.* But then I remember it's Charlie on the other side.

I get up, throw on a bathrobe, and tiptoe out of my room and to Charlie's. I attempt to knock lightly, but his door creaks open under the pressure.

"Charlie?" I whisper.

He's asleep on his back, one arm stretching out from under the comforter and his face relaxed.

"Charlie?" I say louder.

He mumbles and turns onto his side. The bedding is up to his chin and I have to admit, it's adorable how tucked in he is.

I stand by the side of the bed and lean over, placing a hand on his torso. The quilt is lavender and silky under my palm.

Charlie still doesn't wake up, but I nearly jump out of my skin when his hand hits the back of my knee.

"Mmm," he grunts. "Come back to bed."

I freeze. Who does he think is waking him up? My heart, the stupid, careless thing that it is, aches. Just because Charlie didn't bring anyone to Christmas doesn't mean he's not dating or sleeping with someone . . . or multiple someones. Charlie is objectively hot, and women love tech bros—just look at my boss, who was often on hottest-bachelor lists—and I'm sure he's had plenty of sex since we've broken up and it's too early in the morning and I'm unprepared to think so much about Charlie's sex life before I've had my coffee and—

"Bea," Charlie says, louder this time. "Come back to bed."

His hand slides up the back of my thigh, beneath my robe, almost to my butt, and squeezes the muscle there.

Me?

I look down at Charlie. His eyes are still closed, and the fingers wrapped around me relax as he falls back into sleep.

Why would Charlie say my name?

His phone, which had stopped buzzing on the nightstand, starts up again.

I shove his arm away and then push his shoulder hard enough to flip him to his back and jolt him awake.

He blinks up at me in surprise.

"Charlie, your phone's ringing," I snap.

I turn and stomp out of the room, mad at myself for getting so flustered over something so stupid.

10

CHARLIE

"How is it that I'm the only one in our family who doesn't know how to ski?" Bea asks. She's dressed in navy snow pants and Naomi braided her hair this morning after breakfast while Bea applied some makeup.

We're at Sirens' Valley Lodge on Sunday morning, and it's taken us almost an hour and a half to get everyone ski passes and rentals going. I'm sweating in my layers, having made sure everyone's stuff got carried from the gear counter to a cluster of picnic tables where most of the family is sitting and having an early lunch from the snack bar.

The call that woke Bea up was Arlo. He had a few questions for me about the due diligence—mostly around my sales staff contracts—and wanted to catch me before the day got started. He'd been just as surprised as I was that I'd slept in past seven—vacation was getting to me.

But talking to Arlo first thing in the morning was exactly the wake-up call I needed to get some work done before the house was awake, and I was feeling productive already today.

"Honey, you're not the only one." Mom pats Bea's hand.

"Okay, but you're choosing not to ski, and that's totally

fair. But like, we went to Pithole for years and no one ever skied there."

"That's because Pithole was a pit hole," Yvette says.

That's not entirely accurate because my dad grew up in the area and that's where he learned to ski, but Dad doesn't defend his hometown, either because he's warmed up to the luxuries of Here, New York, or because the chicken tenders basket he got is getting cold and he's too busy eating it.

"Well, you know we went to Maine for our thirtieth anniversary," Erik says, slinging an arm around Jody and pulling her into a snuggle.

"I won the over-sixty beginner race that week," Jody adds proudly.

"Fine. And you two I get"—Bea points between Yvette and Lance, who live in Chicago—"because lake-effect snow and Montana boy. And I know Naomi went with friends from her running club. But you two?" Now she points at Kayla and Jasper.

"What, are you saying Black people can't ski?" he teases.

"No, I'm saying someone who grew up in Louisiana and now lives in Florida doesn't have many opportunities to learn to ski."

"My athletic prowess knows no bounds."

"I think the real question," Yvette interjects, "is why don't *you* know how to ski?"

"Well." Bea frowns and picks at her french fries. "I guess I haven't had anyone to go with."

There's a heavy moment of silence around the table while Erik and Jody give each other concerned looks.

"Well, that's going to change today," I say. "You've got a lesson in half an hour."

Bea looks up. "Wait, what? I have to take a lesson? Why can't one of you teach me?" She looks pointedly at her sisters.

Kayla holds up her hands. "Last time I tried to teach you something you told me I made you look like a vampire."

"You had used a concealer two shades too pale and black mascara!"

"I was eighteen and in beauty school!"

"Girls, enough," Jody says.

"Dad?" Bea asks.

"Sorry, pumpkin. I've got my own snow bunny to keep track of. Besides, you know what they call a slow skier? A slope-poke."

There's a collective groan.

Bea pouts. "So I'm the remedial skier. Great."

"You didn't ask Charlie to teach you," Kayla says, lifting an eyebrow.

I interrupt. "She doesn't have to because she's taking a lesson and I've already lined up the instructor." My plan is to hit the slopes with my dad and Bea's parents for a while and then check on Bea after her lesson and see if she wants to do the bunny slope. She'll do way better with a professional ski instructor than with me anyway. I'm good enough for a small-town ski resort, but she'll get more out of a paid lesson.

Besides, I'm happy to treat.

Bea and Naomi pester Jasper on his skiing skills while everyone else finishes their food, and then we hit the slopes. I'm in line for the ski lift with the rest of the family, but I can see Bea over by the bunny slope. I keep glancing over as we get closer to the lift, growing more and more concerned by what I see.

The ski instructor is a young guy, maybe early twenties, and something he says makes Bea laugh. Her dimples come out in full force and he touches her arm. Objectively, he's a good-looking guy, but he's too young for her, right?

What interest would she have in dating a college kid?

"Okay, we're up," Jody says, followed by a "weeeeee" as she slides down the tiny incline to get in position for the chair. Dad and Erik got on the previous one while I wasn't paying attention, so now I'm going to be riding with Bea's mom.

I cast one more glance at Bea—she's *still* laughing? Are they actually going to get any skiing in or are they just going to flirt?

The chair knocks into the back of my knees and I pinwheel my arms to keep my balance, sending one of my poles flying, and I get a solid seat on the bench bare milliseconds before my skis come off the ground.

"Shit, sorry!" I shout down to the rapidly shrinking lift attendant. "I'll come back for it!"

Who knows if they heard me, but I'll take the easiest run down and should be fine with just one pole.

"You okay?" Jody grins at me. I've always liked Bea's mom, though I don't spend a lot of time alone with her.

"Yup, fine, sorry. I didn't mean to scare you."

"You didn't. Seems like you are distracted this year, though."

I hum and glance back toward the bunny slope, but I can't make out Bea and her ski instructor.

"Charlie?"

"Right, sorry. Yeah, kind of distracted, I guess."

"Does my daughter have anything to do with your move to New York?"

Jody studies me as I struggle to come up with an answer. The Cummingses have always treated me like the son they never had, and I hate that I signed an NDA and can't tell the whole truth. "Not directly," I finally say, "but it'll be a nice side benefit, I hope."

"Well, you sure are pulling out all the stops this year. Seems like your company is doing really well." Jody kicks her ski, nonchalant about the financial meddling that I've already fought with my dad about on this trip.

"What do you mean?"

Jody smiles. "Well, I figured our trip was being subsidized somehow, because there's no way that what Erik and I paid covers a majority of that house."

"Maybe we got a good deal."

"Ah, yes, that's what it was. You're a prime negotiator."

We come to the top of the mountain and then we're too busy skiing to talk about anything other than the trails. It's a smaller resort than I've been used to out west, so by the time my watch alarm goes off to signal the end of Bea's lesson, I've done all the runs and know exactly where to take her next.

I come off the front black diamond and slide toward the bunny slope. I scan the people coming down its gentle hill and spot Bea before she spots me. She's smiling and confident, skiing alongside her instructor.

Spotting me, she waves and points her skis in my direction. She slides to a halt a little short and uses her poles to push herself forward before lifting her goggles onto her helmet.

"Hi," she says, breathless and smiling. Her cheeks are rosy pink from the cold and exertion.

"Hey, how was your lesson?"

"Great! Great, right?" She turns to the ski instructor.

"Yeah, she did a great job. I'm Gavin." He offers his hand and I shake it.

"Charlie."

"Okay, well, Bea, any questions for me?"

"No, I'm ready."

"Great, glad to hear it. If you want to book another session, I'm happy to work with you on the bigger slopes. But I'm sure your partner can take over from here."

"He's not my partner," she blurts.

"Not anymore," I say. "We were together. Before."

"A long time ago." Bea's smile is gone and she's widening her eyes at me, the universal sign for *Shut up.*

Except I kinda can't. "Not that long ago."

"Eight years is a long time, Charlie," Bea says, an edge in her voice.

"Well, okay then." Gavin chuckles uncomfortably. "Have a

great time up on the mountain, Bea. Charlie." He nods good-bye, and in a smooth move, presses the tip of one pole to the binding, which pops one foot out, then that foot steps on the other binding and he's free. He nudges his toes under the base and kicks each ski up and hoists them over his shoulder.

"Show off," I mutter.

Bea glares at me. "Not a long time?" she echoes.

"Feels like yesterday," I say cheerfully.

———

"Is this a green?" Bea asks while looking directly at the sign with the big green dot on it.

"Yup," I assure her.

"But is it, like, an *easy* green?"

I laugh. "Yes, this is the easiest of easy greens. I did all the runs today and this one is the best."

She's still skeptical. "It looks really steep."

"It's not that bad. And I'll be right here with you."

"Okay."

We stand there a moment, other groups getting off the ski lift and gliding past us down the hill.

"Do you want me to go first?"

She nods.

"Okay. Goggles on." She follows instructions and I push myself over the small lip. I *swoosh-swoosh-swoosh* and slide to a stop fifty feet or so from Bea. "Your turn," I shout back.

Bea shuffles her skis over to the edge and braces herself. Carefully, she tips over the side, but her skis are angled in. She's pizza-ing down the slope, but picking up speed.

"French fry!" I shout at her.

"What?" She's going faster now, and her mouth is making an O, and not the good kind.

"You're pizza-ing! You need to french fry!"

Bea passes me too fast, unable to stop. "I'M NOT

HUNGRY!" she shouts, but there's fear laced in her voice. She's out of control and zooming past.

A kid no older than five whips by me and then zips past Bea too close for comfort. Bea jerks and loses the battle against her skis. They cross over each other and she tumbles down with a shriek.

Complete yard sale.

11

BEA

I can't see anything but blue sky. The snow beneath me is icy and hard and I'm pretty sure I got some down my pants.

One ski is facing the wrong direction and it's wildly uncomfortable. Must fix that ASAP . . . when my heart stops feeling like it's going to explode out of my chest.

A red helmet and yellow reflective goggles appear. Gloves come up and remove the goggles to reveal Charlie looking at me with concern in his eyes.

"You okay?" He's kneeling next to me, which must mean he took his skis off.

"Maybe?"

There's a *whoosh* as someone swerves past. I better get up before I get run over.

Charlie must have the same idea, because he grabs my hand and peels my fingers off the pole grip. Huh. I was still hanging on. Oh wait, just with one hand. My other hand clenches on air.

Next, he moves down to my boots and I feel the tug as he pushes hard on the release button of my ski. With a snap, it comes undone, and my left leg can move freely.

When he moves to the right and pushes, a sharp pain shoots up from my ankle and I cry out.

"Shit. Bea?"

"I'm fine, I'm fine. I think I tweaked something?"

"Okay, why don't we get you up on your other foot and untwist this one?"

Charlie stands over me, reaching down to grab me beneath my armpits and haul me to my feet. My gloves scramble for purchase until I snag his pockets and hold on.

We're a tripod, him bracing himself in the snow and me leaning into him while the occasional skier passes in a *whoosh*.

"Okay, just . . . hang on." Charlie grunts and shifts as he tries to maneuver his foot around to the back of my boot and apply enough pressure to snap the ski off.

"Get a room," someone shouts as they pass, the Doppler effect in full gear so that the R is loud and the *ooooom* is elongated.

I giggle. To be fair, Charlie, wrapped around me like this and stomping on the release does look like he's humping me.

Finally the ski comes off and without my foot, it hits the snow and slides down a few feet. Charlie and I teeter for a moment before we both lose the fight and come crashing down onto the snow.

Somehow I end up on top of Charlie, our helmets whacking each other before my head bounces off to one side.

Gah.

Charlie's helmet turns toward me and this is the closest I've been to his eyes in a long time. I'd forgotten how green they are right around his irises.

"You okay?" he asks.

"Fine." Well, I've now fallen twice in five minutes, and neither time could be counted as sexy at all. I roll off Charlie.

He sits up and points at me. "Stay there."

He gathers up our skis and poles and moves them to the side of the slope and into the woods where no one is going to run them over. Then he's back in front of me, holding out his hands.

"Can you stand?"

I grip both his hands and rise on one leg. Once I'm stable, I test putting my weight on my right leg.

I wince and Charlie frowns.

There's no way I can ski down like this.

"All right, let's get you to the side so we don't get run over and I'll go for help." Charlie offers me his hand again.

"Help?" I yelp. "What kind of help?" Together we shuffle (him) and hop (me) to the tree line.

"It's not a big mountain but it would probably take us hours to get down like this. They have snowmobiles for people who get injured."

I'm just about to sit down again when I hear the sharp, crisp noise of someone expertly stopping on snow behind us. "You folks okay?"

Together, Charlie and I turn to see an employee of the resort stopped a few feet away. He's wearing a bright red "Sirens' Valley Lodge" jacket with a big white cross on it.

Below his ski goggles is an amiable smile on a chiseled jaw covered in scruff. He lifts his ski goggles to the top of his helmet and his eyes are gorgeous blue.

Jesus, what is in the water here? Between him and my cute instructor, there's plenty of potential small-town romance. If only I didn't look like a doofus. And if only Charlie would *go away*.

"She fell and hurt her ankle," Charlie says.

The smile disappears and the handsome rescuer slips into professional mode. "Why don't I radio for the toboggan and we can get you down the slope, ma'am?"—*MA'AM? I just got MA'AM'd by Hot Ski Rescue Guy??*—"It'll remove you from the path of traffic, and I'm an EMT. Once we get you out of your boots, I can look at that foot."

"Okay, sounds good." My voice is weak, and I'm not sure

if it's because my foot is starting to throb or I just got ma'am'd at the age of twenty-eight.

Hot Ski Rescue Guy pulls out a walkie-talkie-radio thing and turns away to talk into it. Charlie leans his head close to mine. "Did he just call you ma'am?"

I snort-laugh, almost making us lose our balance again. "Forget making my butt look big, apparently my ski outfit makes me look old."

Within a minute, there's a snowmobile with a toboggan pulled up next to us, facing uphill. "Your chariot awaits," Charlie mutters to me.

The two ski resort staff members help me settle into the toboggan and tuck my equipment next to me. Facing this way, I can see the top of the chairlift and watch people at the start of the run.

Wow, I did not make it far at all.

The toboggan starts up and next thing I know we're running down the trail. I turn slightly, and can see Charlie and Hot Ski Rescue Guy skiing easily behind us, *swoosh-swoosh-swooshing* from left to right. Show-off. I roll my eyes, which I'm sure Charlie can't see through my goggles, but he must be able to guess what I did because he sticks his tongue out at me.

I flip him off and he laughs.

Down at the base, we pull up right by the ski lift so that *everyone* waiting in line can see me get helped out of the toboggan and hobble into the lodge.

Neither Hot Ski Rescue Guy nor Charlie offers to carry me in.

Bummer.

Hot Ski Rescue Guy—whose actual name is Miguel but I like Hot Ski Rescue Guy, or HSRG for short, better—inspects my ankle, declares it a slight sprain, and recommends a RICE regimen—rest, ice, compress, and elevate.

Naomi arrives. Charlie called her when we got to the

lodge, and she does the same evaluation and tells me I'll have to be a lazy bum for a few days.

Then Mom and Dad swing by and I have to hear Charlie tell the entire story for the third time. It's getting more elaborate with every retelling. I lived it, can we just not? I can literally feel myself melting into the couch from a mixture of embarrassment and exhaustion, and Charlie must read something on my face.

"Okay, I'm going to take her back to the house," he says, breaking up my parents fretting over whether there's enough ice on my ankle. "Y'all should get back on the ski slope and enjoy the rest of your day."

"Are you sure?" Mom asks him, and then looks at me. "Are *you* sure?"

"Yes, I'll be fine."

Mom hears the irritation in my voice and pats my hand. "Okay. Text us if you need anything."

Charlie helps me hobble to my rental car and takes the keys, driving us back to the house. He settles me on the couch, hands me my e-reader, and immediately steals my car and goes to the store.

"Here," he says, dumping four bags from the local Shop-Rite on the coffee table in front of me. He digs a few saggy blue things out of one bag, and I recognize those flexible ice packs. He disappears into the kitchen, putting them in the freezer, and I poke through the rest of the bags. An ankle brace, bandages, painkillers, and Sour Punch Straws, my favorite movie-watching candy. There's also a paperback book—when was the last time I bought a paperback?—and a few magazines.

Including a magazine that boasts "Best Cardio Tips for Women over 50" and "What to Eat During Menopause."

"Is this an old lady joke?" I ask, pretending to huff about it.

"No ma'am," Charlie says with a straight face. He dodges

when I throw the magazine at him. When his laughter dies down, he asks, "Do you want to shower?"

I look down at myself. I am still in my ski outfit, which swishes every time that I move, and now that I think about it, the back of my neck and my underwear are still slightly damp from the snow getting down it.

"Good idea." Pajamas sound great right now.

Charlie helps me up. We make it up three steps before deciding that it would just be easier to bring my stuff to me and I'll shower downstairs. Charlie grabs my stuff and after I thank him, we stand there staring at each other in the small bathroom.

12

BEA

"WHAT?" I ASK.

"I'm helping you."

"Excuse me?"

He points down at my offending ankle. "You aren't supposed to put weight on it. How do you plan to shower?"

"Carefully."

He makes a face at me.

"I'll be naked!"

"Come on. I've seen you naked before."

"That was a long time ago."

"Don't worry, I'm sure your breasts still look amazing in your old age."

"Charlie!"

"Bea!" The corner of his lip quirks up.

I glare at him.

"Safety first," he admonishes.

"You're annoying."

"I don't care."

I glare at him some more.

"Would you rather me call your sister or your mom?" This question isn't teasing but genuine.

Now he's all mature, and I have to grow up too.

"No, it's fine. Just . . . don't look."

"Okay, how about I stand right here"—he moves to right next to the tub—"and I'll even close my eyes." He demonstrates, covering his eyes with his hands.

"Fiiiiiiine."

Charlie drops his arm and I unzip my jacket, the thin one I normally wear when I go for a run. Then I peel off the tank top and sports bra.

Charlie whistles, but when I glance up his hand is still covering his eyes, right above his big, stupid grin.

I whack him with my sports bra before throwing it on the pile.

Okay, pants now.

I sit on the toilet to peel off the rest. I unwrap the basic bandage that the medic put on my ankle and toss it in the trash. Then I hobble over to Charlie fully nude and rest my hand on his shoulder. "Okay, now what?"

"Hm. Maybe sit on the edge of the tub and I'll get the water started."

I sit down, stretching out my leg while Charlie fumbles with the faucet. I move my foot this way and that, inspecting it. There's a bit of a twinge but I don't think there's any swelling beneath the compression lines from the bandage.

Steam billows out from behind the shower curtain. "Ready?" I ask.

"Ready," Charlie confirms. His eyes are still closed, though now his hand isn't covering them anymore. He holds out his hand instead. "Here, give me your hand and stand up."

I do, and with his help I stand and maneuver around. Charlie ends up holding on to my shoulders while I face away from the showerhead and wash my hair. Then he holds one hand again while I use my loofah to suds up.

Throughout this, I keep glancing at Charlie's face. Sometimes his lips twitch, possibly trying not to laugh or smile. But mostly he's just quiet and relaxed.

He's wearing one of those waffle-style long-sleeve shirts, and he's rolled it up past his elbows, though his sleeves are pretty soaked.

Finally, I turn the water off. "All clean," I tell him. He helps me sit and spin my legs out before retrieving the towel and holding it out for me.

I could take the towel from him and dry off. I *should* dry myself off. I could sit here on the tub and wrap myself up, and he could open his eyes . . .

Instead, I hobble into the center of the towel and Charlie wraps it around me. I grip the top and curl it around myself.

"Can I open my eyes now?" It starts with a teasing tone, but in the silence afterward, it fades to something else.

He's so close right now, and I study his face in a way I haven't in a long time.

Charlie's skin is darker than mine, a natural golden tan he gets from Susan. His eyebrows and hair are dark and thick, like hers too. A small mole on the right side of his face just under his eye is one I kissed a lot. Those features haven't changed.

But there are new things, or maybe things I've forgotten about. A small scar on his upper lip, slightly darker bags under his eyes that make me think of how little sleep he got sometimes when he was away at college. I don't know when the last time he shaved was, but he's past a five-o'clock shadow now, the stubble on his jaw and upper lip thick.

I haven't answered his question, and he hasn't opened his eyes either. Instead, he runs his hands up and down my arms and my back, drying me off under the big, fluffy towel.

He gently tugs the towel out of my grip and it falls, catching on his hands. They move down my hips, rubbing slow circles down the front of my legs, and Charlie crouches. I hear his breath catch as his hands shift to behind me, drying off the back of my legs.

He's on his knees in front of my naked body, his eyes tightly closed, taking care of me.

There's a heavy moment, and Charlie clears his throat before standing. He wraps me tightly in the towel, firmly tucking the end in at my back.

"Can I open my eyes now?" He says it so softly I feel it deep inside my chest.

Where he's already broken me once before.

I look away, catch sight of a second towel for my hair, and hop toward it. "Yup," I chirp, trying to sound every ounce of casualness that I don't feel.

The mood shifts and at my request, Charlie leaves me to get dressed myself, wiggling my sleep shorts up over my hips while I balance on the toilet again. Back out in the living room, I tell him my ankle is throbbing a bit, so I lie down and close my eyes while he carefully wraps it and lays the ice pack on it.

It does throb now that I'm paying attention to it, so it's not entirely an excuse.

I keep my eyes closed while Charlie pulls a blanket up to my chin, and when I crack them open a few minutes later, he's in one of the armchairs on his laptop, presumably working.

I don't have to fake a nap for long before the door opens and our boisterous family comes rolling in. The moms cluck over me and Naomi rewraps the bandage. We graze on leftovers and cheese platters for dinner, spread out between the living room, dining room, and kitchen.

I've got a text from Marco, a picture of him and Brin with a ridiculously large pile of wrapped presents in our living room.

BEA

What are you two up to?

MARCO

Getting paper cuts, apparently.

He sends me another pic of his thumb, with a bright red slash across it. We chat for a bit, him telling me that the snow has basically turned to slush in the city, and I send him a picture of our idyllic, fresh-snow-covered backyard. He makes no mention of the kiss from yesterday, so I'm left to wonder what happened.

My family had a great time at the mountain, and they make plans to go out again the next morning. Naomi helps me up the stairs, and back down the stairs in the morning, where I settle on the couch again.

"Are you sure you don't want one of us to stay behind?" Mom perches on the arm and strokes my hair while she asks. "You know I'd stay behind if you wanted some company."

I love my mom but spending a whole day alone with her probably means doing something energetic, and since I can't put weight on my foot, that probably means we'll watch a movie that Mom talks through while she crochets in the armchair or something. Or she'd spend the morning baking cookies and shouting at me from the kitchen while I try to read.

"I'll be fine," I promise. "I have an audiobook I have to finish before it goes back to the library."

"Anything good?"

My mom is mostly a nonfiction reader, so we don't have a lot of overlap in our reading choices. "It's about a hockey player," I hedge. It *is* about a hockey player, but it's a smutty romance.

She hums, uninterested in sports. To be fair, I'm uninterested in sports too, but not when it comes to fictional hockey players.

"Besides, you promised Susan you would go snow tubing with her."

Mom grins. "I did. That way Gary and Erik can go hit the black diamonds." Her smile changes, an eyebrow raising. "You know, Charlie would stay behind if you asked him to."

My cheeks heat, thinking of the way Charlie took care of me yesterday. "He's enjoying skiing," I say firmly. "And his day was cut short to take care of me. I promise, Mom, I'll be fine."

She fusses a bit more and then makes a sandwich for me for lunch before she goes, which I'll probably ignore in favor of cookies and the Sour Punch Straws.

Finally I have the house to myself. I lie on the couch and eat cookies, listening to my audiobook until I realize I've completely lost the plot and must have fallen asleep. I go back a few chapters and take out my headphones. They've been in my ears long enough that they are getting uncomfortable, and if I'm going to fall into a sugar coma, I'd rather do so unencumbered by headphones.

My audiobook starts getting really spicy.

"He shoves his hands up my skirt and my back hits the cold metal of the locker. 'There's no one here, so I get to make you be as loud as I want.' His fingers move from my silken entrance up to my clit, where he circles with his callused fingertip."

I'm so wrapped up in listening that I must not hear the door open, and the first cue that I'm not alone is a flash of movement above me.

I jolt upright and twist around.

Charlie's standing at the entrance to the room, his mouth open and clutching imaginary pearls, trying to pass for shocked and scandalized while holding back his laughter.

My audiobook drones on. "'Ryan, what are you doing?' The words come out breathy. 'I'm getting you ready to take my cock like a good puck bunny,' he responds."

I scramble for my phone and in my fluster, I drop it, sending it skidding under the couch.

"Nooooo." I flip myself upside down, peering into the dark, where the audiobook continues to play over the sound of Charlie's mirth.

"'Oh Ryan,' I moan. 'I can't . . . I need you inside me. Make me come.'"

I flip up my head to glare at Charlie. "Shut up and help me," I demand.

"Like she needs his help to get off?" Charlie chuckles, but he crouches down at the end of the couch and reaches underneath. He pulls out my phone and a fistful of dust bunnies.

"Bleh." I make a face.

"Hey, you're the one who's listening to it."

"Not that!" I roll my eyes. "Your hand is all gross." I finally pause the book and the sex scene cuts off.

Charlie wiggles his fingers and stands, walking into the kitchen to wash his hands. He's still in his under layers, his hair mussed and sweaty from his helmet.

"What are you doing here anyway?" I shout over the sound of the sink, praying we can just ignore the broadcasted smut.

"I wanted some of Jasper's fried chicken for lunch."

Uh-huh. Sure. "It's—" I check the time while Charlie dries his hands. "Two thirty."

"Yeah, and I'm starving." He digs through the fridge, pulling out wrapped plates and baking dishes. I hobble over to the counter. After last night's grazing, we're almost out of leftovers and the fridge is looking pretty bare again, so we might need to run to the store soon. But for now, there's still a few pieces of chicken and a few bags of microwave-ready veggies.

Charlie stretches on his toes, exaggeratedly looking at the coffee table and my plate of cookie crumbs and half-full bag of Sour Punch Straws. "Why don't I heat up enough for you too?"

Even though it's cold, I can smell the breading on the chicken and there's still one leg quarter left, calling my name. *Eat me, Bea. Even fresh out of the fridge, I'm delicious.* "I suppose."

Charlie grins and turns on the oven. Oh yay, *hot* fried chicken. "I'm going to go shower. I'll throw the chicken in when I get back down."

"Yeah. You stink."

He winks and climbs the stairs two at a time.

I hop back to the couch and flop onto it. I just know that five, ten, fifteen years from now, I'll have a sleepless night and remember that time Charlie overheard my smutty romance novel.

My thoughts are interrupted by a knock at the door. I sit up. Who could that be?

Maybe one of my sisters forgot the code to the door. I get to my feet—well, foot—and hop my way out of the living room and into the front hallway. I didn't think it was unnecessarily long, but now that I'm hobbling down it, it seems to stretch forever.

Just as I get to the foot of the stairs, I hear a beep and the lock slides open. I reach for the handle but miss as the front door swings toward me and I lose my balance, falling directly into the arms of a flannel-wearing, handsome stranger.

13

CHARLIE

THE STEAM FROM THE SHOWER BILLOWS OUT INTO THE BATHROOM as I pull the curtain back. The bathroom is small—cozy—and there's stuff strewn all over the place, even though at least half of Bea's stuff is in the downstairs bathroom temporarily. My toiletries have mingled with Bea's and Naomi's and I'm pretty sure someone used my toothpaste last night, which is fine.

When I'd first seen the stuff spread out, I'd wanted to reach out and touch every item and see if I could tell if it was Bea's or her sister's. Yesterday made me realize how far off my guesses were.

I just reach for a towel and scrub my face and hair. Moving down my chest, I don't have the scrape of dry towel on wet skin in my ears and I can hear voices downstairs.

I smile, thinking about Bea's audiobook, and catching her lying on the couch, eyes closed and her arms crossed. Her thumb was just lightly stroking her upper arm, and I wonder if she even knew she was doing it.

I scrub my junk, drying my upper thighs and my balls, when I hear a shriek and freeze.

It doesn't sound like an audiobook—it sounds like Bea.

And a man's voice answers.

I wrap the towel around myself, tucking the corner in as I fling the door open and hustle down the hall to the stairs. The voice gets louder—it's definitely a man and he's definitely *in here.*

The stairs are carpeted and I take them two at a time. I grip the banister to swing toward the living room and skid in, the rug beneath me sliding just enough that I lose my balance and have to catch myself—and my towel—before I see that there is a man in here, and he and Bea are both smiling . . . or at least they were until I ran in like a berserker.

He's got an arm slung over her shoulders and is lowering her onto the couch. I'm spared barely a glance by both of them as he gently releases her and she settles into the cushion.

"There," he says, dusting his hands off. "Can I get you anything else?"

Bea smiles up at him like he hung the moon. Then she points with one hand toward the pillow on the floor. "Could you get me that pillow? I knocked it off when I was answering the door."

"Of course."

I watch like a chump, a small puddle of water dripping onto the rug, as this stranger helps her, lifting her foot up and fluffing the pillow carefully before placing her foot back down.

All things Bea insisted on handling herself this morning.

"Thank you so much."

The guy smiles right back at her as if they are the only two people in the world. He's about our age, with thick sandy-brown hair that flops to one side and a lean build. The sleeves of his flannel are rolled up and he's wearing boots and jeans.

"You're very welcome," he says, and stands, turning to face me.

"Hey, I'm Kit Hutchinson." He offers me a hand and a

wide smile, completely unfazed by the fact that I'm wearing nothing but a towel.

I squint at his hand, then squint at him. "Who are you, Kit?"

He retracts his hand and chuckles good-naturedly. "There seems to have been a mix-up. I'm with the rental company, and we offer a light cleaning for our guests every few days. I wasn't expecting anyone to be home."

Oh, I had responded to an email from the rental company saying we'd be out skiing. My mouth opens but Bea interrupts. "Are you a local?"

"Indeed I am." Kit puts his hands in his jeans pockets in an almost *aw shucks* move and then sits on the coffee table to be eye level with Bea. "Born and raised."

I move closer and cross my arms. I'm going for looming. *We don't need a cleaning service, surely you're a busy man, move along now.* He doesn't take the hint.

Bea glances at me—or maybe it's a glare—and then asks him some questions about the area. He's a walking travel guide, suggesting places to eat and telling her she's got to come back in the summer to hike.

Finally, Kit claps his hands on his thighs and stands. "Well, unless you need anything, I better get going."

"Well, actually . . ." Bea starts. She smiles up at Kit. "Could you chop some firewood for us?"

He chuckles. "Been enjoying the fireplace? It's very romantic." He winks at her.

What am I, invisible? Chopped liver? I'm *right here.*

"We don't need more firewood," I say to deaf ears. Bea definitely glares at me this time.

Kit saunters over to the window to gaze outside. He turns back to Bea, his brow wrinkled but still a teasing smile on his lips. "There *is* plenty of wood outside. It should be enough to last the rest of your visit, even if you use both the fireplace and the firepit every night."

"We eat a lot of s'mores," she confesses. She's flirting with him!

"There's an axe in the shed, so it won't take me long to replenish your supply. You can just call me if you need more."

"Sounds great, Kit."

Bea picks up her phone and Kit rattles out his number. She texts him, and there's an answering ding in his back pocket.

"All right, well, enjoy your time in Here, and if you need anything, let me know." He smiles at Bea, nods at me, and then shows himself out.

Bea watches him leave the room and then sighs when the door closes.

"Chopping wood, really?" I ask.

She picks up her headphones from the table and shrugs, not even bothering to look at me while she puts them in. "What? It would have been hot."

My back teeth grind, and I spin around and stomp upstairs.

Hot? I'll show her hot.

14

BEA

Wow.

It takes everything in me not to watch Charlie walk away, the white towel wrapped around his cute butt straining.

It's a good thing Charlie has been using laser death ray eyes on Kit. He was too focused on the hunk of small-town charm in the living room to catch me staring at him.

Charlie sure has grown up. Obviously I knew he was attractive. There's a vast difference between the twenty-year-old Charlie of our breakup and the twenty-eight-year-old Charlie of now, but the changes that I've noticed have all been, well, pretty vague from the neck down. It's not like we're spending the holidays wearing bathing suits, and while I knew that Charlie had bulked out, I hadn't realized the extent of it.

Charlie is *ripped*. His pecs are solid and firm, the soft-looking patch of chest hair between them is thicker, and he has a V-cut.

A V-cut.

What happened to the nerdy boy I fell in love with?

When I snapped out of my shock, I realized that Charlie was jealous. It wasn't just stranger danger and concern for my well-being with an unknown man in the house. It was an *Excuse me, she's mine.*

The moment I'd fallen into Kit's arms I'd thought, *Wow, he's hot.* It may not have been sexy or graceful on my part, but it *was* a fantasy come true. And now I have his number.

I should call Kit. This is exactly what I want, right? A small-town guy to sweep me off my feet?

And yet . . .

I hate myself for even thinking of it, but Charlie, even after breaking my heart all those years ago, still pulls me to him like a magnet.

And now that I've seen most of grown-up Charlie, I'm even more attracted to him than before.

I realize I've been staring into space with my headphones on and I haven't even hit play yet on my audiobook. Charlie is thumping around upstairs, maybe throwing a tantrum, but that's fine, whatever.

I hit play and pull up a game on my phone.

I make it through a few rounds of Sudoku on the hard level and another chapter of my audiobook in which the characters have a very hot round in the locker room shower before movement catches my gaze again. Charlie stalks through the living room, a determined glint in his eye. He's dressed now, wearing jeans and a hoodie.

I pause my audiobook and sit up. "What are you doing?"

"You'll see," he says, disappearing into the kitchen, and a few seconds later the door to the backyard slams. I scramble to my feet and hop over to the big picture window, the one Kit was just looking out of to check on the firewood pile.

Charlie tugs his shoes on and walks out to the shed, opening the door and disappearing inside.

"What in the world?" I wonder under my breath.

Holding the door open, I shuffle out and onto the porch. I have a sweater on already, and it's sunny out, so the nip of cold in the air is dulled.

Charlie reemerges from the shed with an axe.

My hands go to my hips. "What the hell are you doing?"

Charlie walks toward the pile of logs, points the axe and his gaze at me. "I'm going to chop you some wood."

That intention in his eyes and the handling of the weapon make me shiver. Yowsa.

Except this is ridiculous. I shake myself and make my voice even sterner. "You are going to lose a finger. You've never chopped wood before in your life."

There's a big stump by the log pile, crisscrossed with notches from the axe. Charlie lifts his weapon and with a *thunk* drives it into the flat top.

My heart flutters.

"I watched some videos."

I take a minute to parse the words. "You *watched some videos.* Charlie! This is ridiculous!"

He ignores me and picks up a log from one end of the woodpile. I hadn't looked closely at it, but one side of the pile has big round logs, literally just chunks of tree, and the other has wedges of wood ready for a fireplace or pit.

So I guess this is happening. The log is on his shoulder and he takes a few steps and bends down to set it on the stump. It's short and fat. Like, really thick. But, wait. It's not as thick as the stump.

What is thick for a log? I don't know! I'm a city girl!

Once the log is stable, Charlie grabs the handle of the axe, pulling it from the flat top, and hefts it over his shoulder with both hands. Before I can even blink, he's swung the axe down and hit the log.

It, um, doesn't do much. But it also doesn't bounce off and hit his face or go wildly for left field into his femur, so that's something.

His next swing is more confident. It goes further into the log, making an enormous crack. Then he doesn't quite hit it right. But finally, the fourth swing splits the log in half and the force of Charlie wrenching the axe out causes the two halves to fall to the side.

He resets one and chops it. Then the other. Then he grabs a new log and starts over.

This is ridiculous. "I know what you're doing. You're jealous of Kit."

He doesn't answer.

"You know I've been with other people since you, right? Can your macho ego take that?"

After the next log is split, Charlie grunts. "I know you have. And I have too. But you aren't sleeping with Kit."

I cross my arms and glare at him. He doesn't know that while I thought Kit was hot, I was much more distracted by Charlie.

If he knew that, he might stop chopping wood, some cavewoman part of my brain whispers.

"Why am I not sleeping with Kit? Afraid of a little competition? Worried he'll do a better job than you did?"

Now that Charlie's gotten the hang of it, he talks between swings.

"He would." *Grunt.* "He's probably got—" *Grunt.* "—better bedroom skills than I did at twenty." *Grunt.* Charlie pauses, axe dug into a log, to stare at me. "But I've gotten better, and he won't have the connection with you and you know it."

My mouth gapes open. Charlie turns back to his work, wrenching the axe out.

That cavewoman part of my brain is stupefied too. We both watch Charlie chop another log, then—because there is a god and she enjoys the view—Charlie takes off his hoodie. He's wearing a white T-shirt underneath that's already damp from his sweat.

This went from ridiculous to hot too fast. My brain is still tripping on "the connection" as Charlie chops more wood.

I should turn around and go back inside. I should shut my

mouth. Or, you know . . . even blinking my eyes would be good.

Finally, with a great crack, a log splits and Charlie leaves the axe buried in the stump.

His gaze meets mine. My unblinking eyes follow him as he walks toward me, and the smell of him hits me first. Clean sweat, snow, and freshly chopped wood, which I didn't even know had a smell. His skin is sheened with perspiration, a drip of liquid runs down his cheek and he's got chips of wood and splinters all over his body.

He stops so close to me that if I take a deep breath, my breasts would brush against his chest.

Holding my gaze, Charlie's finger comes up and touches my chin, pushing my mouth closed with an audible click. But it doesn't stop there. He keeps pressing, tilting my chin until we are breath to breath.

And there, under those smells of work and man and nature, there's the smell of Charlie. A smell that finally makes my eyes flutter as fast as my heart, the rest of my body catching up to the realization that the years haven't made me any less attracted to him than I was when we were together.

A beat passes, and then Charlie's mouth comes crashing down on mine.

15

CHARLIE

I'M A SWEATING, FILTHY MESS BUT BEA DOESN'T SEEM TO CARE. I know that look in her eyes—eight years later it's still the same.

Or . . . it's been longer than eight years since I've seen her look at me with such desire and need. Too long.

How could I not kiss her?

Bea's mouth opens under mine and her flavor floods me. I want to drink her in, memorize the differences from what I remember.

My finger is still at her chin, feeling the movement of muscles and the shift of her jaw as she kisses me back, that soft spot flexing as her tongue tangles with mine. I let my hand slide down, my fingers brushing over her pulse point and cradling her closer to me. My thumb wanders to the front of her throat and she shivers when I fully grip her.

Bea's wearing black leggings and I bend slightly, gripping the back of her knee and lifting it up. Her leg wraps around my hip, keeping the weight off her injured ankle. Our centers are closer together now, and Bea's hips shift. I need more pressure.

I push, gently, and Bea's hands reflexively come up to

89

grab onto my sides. Her fingers tangle in my shirt as I lift her up and walk us forward, mouths still fused together, until she's against the side of the house and I'm pressed against her.

She gasps when our bodies align and I'm so hard for her it hurts. I can still feel her pulse under my palm, the shift of her swallowing against the pressure.

Her hand wraps around my left forearm and squeezes, and I snap back to focus. I'm hurting her, pressing too hard. Shit.

I let her go and pull back but she protests wordlessly, tugging my hand back. Her eyes are lidded, her cheeks flushed with color.

Fuckity fuck fuck fuck.

My hand wraps back around her neck, pressing just slightly harder and she whimpers, this hot, needy little sound that shoots straight to my cock. I lean back into her body, invading her mouth with my tongue.

My jeans are tight and restrictive, but I bite down on the discomfort because I know that the rough material probably feels amazing through her pants.

She groans and pulls away, breathing hard and tilting her head back. I pulse my hand tighter and shift her head to the side. I trail my lips down her cheek and over my thumb, past the hardness of her jaw and to her earlobe, which I nip.

"You know you're mine, right?" I growl. I pull back, and Bea's eyes are dilated, the blue a light ring around her irises. Her lips are kiss-swollen, her hair ruffled from my hands and the wall behind her.

I'm holding her by her throat, which feels so delicate under my hands—hands that are scratched and roughed up from the axe. Sweat clings to me, though for an entirely different reason now, and I'll probably be sore and have blisters tomorrow, but it was all worth it. I don't feel like myself, and as my hips grind with Bea's and I feel the start of an orgasm building, I realize that I've never been this rough in my life.

Somewhere in the house behind Bea, a door slams.

My gaze snaps to hers and both our eyes widen.

"Hey, who left my chicken out on the counter? And why the hell is the oven on?" Jasper's voice comes from the kitchen.

I drop my hand and set Bea down carefully. Once she's on her feet, she pushes me away. This fragile thing should stay just between us for now. Until I can make it more solid.

Bea straightens her sweater and reties her hair back, not meeting my gaze while I stand frozen like an idiot, still hard in my jeans.

With a brief glance at me, Bea spins and hobbles into the house.

I'VE BARELY SAID TWO WORDS TO BEA SINCE OUR MAKE-OUT session. But I've been thinking about it constantly since then.

Last night, after dinner was over and I could reasonably excuse myself, I went up to my room. I hoped Bea would join me at some point, but she never came. Disappointing, yes. But I had lain in bed, replaying our kiss over and over again. My mind snagged frequently on my hand on her throat; the way her soft skin felt against mine, the tiny movements of her body, the moans that vibrated under my hand. Was it simply me holding her that she liked? Or would she want to go further? Breath play? I went down a rabbit hole on the internet of safe practices until I fell asleep.

It shouldn't surprise me that Bea might have a new interest in the bedroom. I have things I've learned over the years that I wouldn't have even known were on the table when we were teenagers. I want to make sure I do it right, without hurting her but still heightening her pleasure.

Now, though, it's December 22, and that means secret Santa shopping. The eleven of us pile into the three cars, and then we're barreling down the road into town.

I catch up with Arlo via text. He's sent a few messages checking up on me, knowing that holidays can often be stressful and I can tell he's worried about me. His kids made me a Christmas card and his oldest, who's nine, has been playing with drag-and-drop programming, so I message with her until the car slows and I look up.

Brick buildings that probably date back at least a hundred years line the main street of Here. I had read that it was a logging town in the early parts of the last century, and expected to die a slow death as the industry moved on, but then the ski resort opened and the Catskills became a hot spot for tourism, leading to Here's survival.

Many of the buildings hold businesses on the first floor. There are a few restaurants, retail shops, a brewery, and more. A cat in the window above a Vietnamese restaurant makes me think the upper floors are housing.

Should be easy enough to find a gift for Bea.

The cars break apart to find empty parking spots and me, my parents, and Yvette and Lance pour out of the Suburban.

"Have fun, kids," Mom calls, grabbing my father by the hand and tugging him down the street.

Yvette grabs her fiancé's hand and they wander off too, leaving me on my own. I suspect that this year, it'll take longer for us to reconvene, with everyone shopping—or window-shopping—long after they've bought gifts.

Plus, it's already eleven a.m., since getting eleven people up, fed, dressed, and out the door is a herculean feat.

I flip an imaginary coin and head off in one direction. Iron lampposts dot the street, sporting flags for the season. There are Christmas wreaths, reindeer, Stars of David, snowflakes, and more lining the street in bright primary colors. I walk the length of the "downtown" area until the shops thin and give way to houses with bigger lawns, and then I turn around and walk back. I catch sight of my parents popping into a jewelry store and Jasper in line at a coffee shop.

And then I spot Bea. She's standing in front of a real estate office gazing at the for-sale listings.

"House shopping?" I ask when I reach her side. She's by herself and the street is quiet. This is the first time we've been alone since the Great Make-out Session of Yesterday.

I expect her to laugh it off, but instead she tips her head. "Maybe."

I jerk my head in surprise. "Really?"

She shrugs. "Yeah. I'd love to have a little house somewhere quaint. You know, raise kids somewhere they can play."

I swallow hard. A memory hits me—Bea and I talking about the future and her saying she wanted to have a big family like hers. "We grew up just fine in the city."

Bea rolls her eyes. "Our parents raised us in the suburbs of a medium-sized town. We had a big park to run around in and a cul-de-sac where we played games. Can you imagine growing up in a place like this?" She gestures around us. Cars slow at the pedestrian crossing down the street to let old ladies cross, there's a playground I passed two blocks away, and I bet the good citizens of Here don't even lock their doors.

"What would you do for work?"

She laughs. "Who needs an assistant in a town like this? I'd rather be a mom anyway." Bea tosses me a look that clearly says *duh* before sauntering off.

I look at the listings, and then stare past them. The other night I was imagining an alternate universe where Bea was pregnant with my child. How many kids would we have? Three? Four? *Five?*

That's a lot of people to take care of. I'd want Bea to do whatever she wants, whatever makes her happy. Selling the business would take care of that. No one would provide for Bea like I could. Not even Kit-what's-his-face.

I meander a bit more, until finally, I step inside a gift shop. There are shirts hung up on one side pronouncing "You Belong Here" in scripted fonts; "Hereian, Hereigan, and Here-er" all crossed out and "Herevian" with big bold letters and exclamation points; "Proud Herevian" and, my favorite: "Forget Whovians, I'm a Herevian!" with a blue telephone booth.

At the end of an aisle is a spinning postcard rack. With a flick of my finger, I spin it one way until it takes a sudden stop and spins back.

I step out of the aisle. Bea is on the other side.

"Hey, again." *Brilliant opener, Charlie.*

Her lips quirk. "Small towns."

She's playing with the rack, spinning it slightly back and forth.

"Have you called Kit?" I ask.

Bea's eyes snap to mine. In a low voice, she says, "You know I'm not going to call him."

My lips curve in a smile. Her eyes drop to my mouth, and she swallows before looking back up at me.

I take a step closer. Bea's chin tilts up slightly. I let my lips part, and then . . .

"Can I help you two find anything?" A short, older woman pops around the corner.

Bea blinks and clears her throat, stepping away. "Just shopping for secret Santa gifts."

"Oh, how fun. Did you know we have some locally made goat's milk soap? Or how about some strawberry jam?"

I don't know who Bea has for secret Santa, but she tilts her head and asks if they have any other jam flavors, and the woman leads her to a display in the corner. I hang back, checking out a display of magnets, when my eyes fall on the perfect gift for Bea.

WE ALWAYS HAVE AT LEAST ONE DINNER OUT DURING OUR Christmas vacation. In Pithole that meant a 24/7 diner where most of us ordered breakfast for dinner. This year, we've got a reservation for the nicest place in Here, the Vietnamese restaurant on Main Street.

As such, we have dressed accordingly and are converging in the front hallway. Mom has on a flowy emerald dress and she's fussing over Dad's sports coat. I join them in dark gray slacks and an open-collared button-up.

"Charlie," Mom coos. "Don't you look handsome." She reaches up to kiss my cheek, and then swipes away the lipstick left behind with her thumb.

Jasper and Lance are already down, chatting quietly on the couch while Jasper twirls the keys on his finger. Well, Jasper's chatting. Lance is the quietest person I've ever met—both soft-spoken and a man of few words.

Jasper's volunteered to be a designated driver tonight, and I wonder if it's in solidarity with Kayla or to throw off the scent for pregnancy suspicions.

Now that I know Kayla's pregnant, I notice some things that most people would probably miss; she occasionally touches her stomach and often goes to "lie down."

Underneath the Christmas tree is even more stuffed than before—when we got back from shopping, we all took turns wrapping our gifts with one of the three rolls of wrapping paper Erik and Jody brought.

I talk to my parents for a while (Dad and I carefully stay away from financial topics) as people filter in. Bea and Naomi are the last to come down, and when I spot Bea, I'm struck all over again by how gorgeous she is.

Her hair is up in a tight bun, winged eyeliner makes her eyes look even bigger than they are, and a berry lipstick colors her mouth. Her ankle is feeling a lot better, and she was able to walk normally today, though she still iced it and propped it up, so she's wearing ballet flats instead of heels. She's in a simple garnet dress, one that accentuates her waist and has a neckline that cuts across her collarbones . . . against which a familiar necklace lies.

I freeze. That's the necklace I gave her. The last gift before we broke up.

Bea doesn't meet my eyes, and in fact, refuses to look at me as we get herded out the door by Jody, who frets about being late. She pulls Naomi, Yvette, and Lance into her rental car, so I load into my parents' Suburban.

Why is she wearing that necklace? She has a great job and dresses for work all the time. I'm sure she has nicer jewelry than a piece that twenty-year-old me could afford.

Why does she even still own it?

Unless . . . I look at that necklace and can't think of anything but our breakup. What if she does the same? What if she's wearing this necklace to remind herself of how awful the implosion was?

"You okay back there, baby boy?"

Mom's question pulls me out of my thoughts. I've been staring—well, glaring, probably—out the car window at the snow-covered woods and buildings passing by.

"Fine. Why?"

My parents exchange a glance, and I'm glad it's just the three of us in the car.

There's a beat of silence, and then Mom pokes Dad, who sighs. "Have you been spending any time with Bea?"

"Some," I say carefully.

"That's good. Just, uh. Be careful there."

Mom turns in the passenger seat to face me behind her. "We just love you both so much and don't want either of you to get hurt. I feel a change in your aura. And I noticed the necklace." She gives me a pointed look.

"Me too."

We pull into a slanted parking spot on Main Street a few blocks from the restaurant. They've put our big, loud party in a back room and given us two servers. I'm across from Bea, and that means that the whole evening, over platters of spring rolls and steaming bowls of phở, I can see every time she touches the pendant.

Like her sister touching her stomach, Bea has a far-off look when she does it, and to me, it feels like every time she touches the pendant, the string between us grows longer and she gets further and further away.

Until the staff pulls the dishes away and all that's left are our drinks and banana pudding and conversation, and Bea catches me staring at her. Her fingers freeze on the necklace, and after a beat, she lowers it to her chest, her gaze warming and her fingers touching it, not absentmindedly, but reverently.

Beneath the table, something nudges my leg. I stretch my foot out and our shoes align, heel to toe, and Bea smiles at me.

16

BEA

It's time for the secret Santa gifts. We crowd around the living room after getting home from the restaurant. Jasper passes out a tray of sugar cookies and jam prints even though we *just* had dessert, and my dad pours spiked hot cocoas or coffees for anyone who wants one.

The fireplace is crackling and radiating heat, and Lance turns the Christmas tree lights on. It's a Norman Rockwell painting, but with more booze and grown-ass adults.

At the cute little gift shop in town, they had mulberry jam, one of my dad's favorites. The rest of the town was, uh, *interesting*. It's charming, for sure. But, while we were in town, I needed to buy some lipstick—I'd forgotten to pack the shade that I wanted—and couldn't find anything close to the quality I get in the city. I also didn't bump into nearly as many cute men my age as I was hoping. A quick flip through Tinder showed me it was slim pickings. Were they just not on dating apps? Or on different ones, like that farmer dating app?

Everyone in town was really nice though, and I got several compliments on my outfit.

I'd also stopped at a real estate office to look at the listings in the window. I had swooned over a two-story colonial listed at $150 per square foot until I'd noticed that it was on two acres of property. Could I picture myself on a riding lawn mower? No.

Meanwhile, I saw the look on Charlie's face when I came down the stairs, and the way he watched me over dinner. Several times I caught him staring at my chest—not at my boobs, which look amazing, by the way, but I *know* he was staring at the necklace.

Is it wishful thinking that Charlie is more attentive this year? I want so badly for him to be the kind of man I want, but he's not. He's still a workaholic, he's still driven and focused. There's no way he'd move out of the city. He just got there.

At least, that's what my brain thinks. The rest of me—my libido, mainly—thinks, *Bang it out! The sex will probably be amazing.*

I settle into an armchair by the tree, my cocoa with Frangelico in hand, a cinnamon stick poking out of the frothy surface. Once again, Mom pulls out her die and we take turns opening presents.

Some are predictable—Susan gets a geode she oohs and ahhs over, which will undoubtedly go somewhere in her front yard—and some are cheesy and make us all laugh, like the socks Mom gets that say "Bring Me My Wine" on the bottom.

It comes down to me and Kayla, and Mom rolls the die. Even number. My turn.

Lance hands me my gift from under the tree. It's flat, and while the gift is a rectangular shape, the item inside is irregular, the corners of the wrapping paper giving way beneath my fingers.

I flip it over and undo the tape on the bottom, sliding the present out. It's black on one side—a magnet—but when I flip it over, there's a paw print on the other side. My eyebrows draw together. I don't have a dog, have never had a dog . . .

I read the text. Smaller letters at the top spell out "I Love," and beneath it the larger letters spell out "Doodles."

My eyes fly to Charlie's across the room. His hand covers his mouth, his eyes dancing with laughter.

I cover my eyes with my hands, shoulders shaking.

"What? What is it?" Yvette takes the magnet out of my hand. "'I love doodles'?" she reads.

I'm fifteen years old again. Charlie and I are at his house, and his mother has set us up in his room with her colored pencils. This is before they moved away, before Gary lost his job, when they were still our next-door neighbors.

Charlie and I had been working on an assignment for art class to make sketches of everyday objects. We'd done that for a while, drawing still lifes of fruit Susan had arranged or random stuff we'd found in his room.

Until one moment, when I had been leaning over Charlie's paper and had looked up at him. He was right there, our faces so close I could feel his breath on mine.

It smelled like mint gum.

Later he'd told me he was chewing it every time we were going to hang out, hoping that *this* time would be the one that he got the nerve to kiss me.

And, leaning over our artwork, he finally did.

It was my first kiss. I'd had crushes on plenty of boys, but never on Charlie. He was, well . . . Charlie.

That kiss changed everything though. Charlie was safe and my best friend, and one kiss led to more and when we finally broke apart, I was swooning hard.

We didn't talk about it, just blushed and went back to our work. But when we came down the stairs, Susan had asked us if we had done "any good doodles," and Charlie and I had giggled. Yes, yes we had.

Doodles came to mean anything but doodling. I'm sure for a while our parents thought we were really getting into art, until they caught on that we were sneaking off to make out.

Now Charlie and I can't stop laughing, and the rest of the room roll their eyes at us.

"You aren't supposed to know who your secret Santa is," Yvette complains.

I ignore her. There's a rule that you aren't allowed to tell, but there have been a few times over the years for each of us that we could guess who our secret Santa was.

Kayla finally gets to open her present—chocolates made locally—and immediately heads to bed. She's been begging off early almost every night that we've been here, and I wonder if she's feeling okay.

The rest of us pass a bag around for the trash and chat, but every time I look at Charlie, he's watching me. The fire is no longer roaring but glows with hot coals instead, and they add to the warmth in his eyes.

I'm drawn into a conversation with Mom, but Charlie's stare lingers. I can almost read his mind. *If I go upstairs, will you come to my room this time?*

When my mom gets up to refill her wine, Charlie stands too. I think, for a moment, that he's going to go upstairs and I have to make my decision, but instead he makes his way to the tree and sits on the floor, picking up a present.

We do the secret Santa, yes, but also married couples exchange gifts and parents still give their kids (and sons-in-law) presents.

Charlie reads the label. "To Kayla, from Mom and Dad." He carefully shakes it. Nothing. "A book," he guesses.

"My sister has a reputation," I agree. Kayla reads a lot of historical fiction, like Philippa Gregory.

My mom returns with a tumbler of amber liquid. "Charlie," she greets him.

Charlie turns to face her and scoots backward until his back is against the front of my chair. I've crossed my legs, one toe pointing off to the Christmas tree, and the other on the floor. I kicked my shoes off long ago, and Charlie's shoulder brushes my knee.

"How's your work going?" Mom asks.

I should probably listen and see if he mentions anything about advertising or sensors or what-have-you, but Charlie crosses his arms, shifts slightly toward my mom, and his fingers brush against my ankle right by his hip.

And they stay there.

No one can see that Charlie is touching me, and his warm palm slides over the top of my foot. His thumb strokes the inside of my ankle, right above the bone where the skin is soft and sensitive.

I feel drugged. The low lights, the hum of my family, and my full belly give the room a dreamlike quality. Like I've plopped down into a cozy scene of the idyllic family holiday, where the most important thing is not what these people have, but that they have each other.

And I have this man at my feet, and I can so easily see what it would be like to give him a second chance.

By ones and twos, people go off to bed until only Yvette and Lance remain. Charlie and Lance are engaged in a discussion about real estate, since Lance and Yvette are shopping for a house and Charlie just bought his first one—granted, my sister and future brother-in-law are buying a suburban house in Chicago and Charlie's place is the polar opposite. Lance mostly listens and my sister, sitting on the far side of the couch, follows the conversation with bemusement.

Finally, she nudges Lance, and they wish us good night too, my sister giving me a meaningful eyebrow raise. Charlie hasn't moved his hand from my ankle the entire time, but the fact that both of us are stalling . . .

When we're alone, Charlie lets his head fall back against the cushion of the chair. I allow myself to reach down and run my fingers through his thick dark hair.

He hums, almost a purr, and rolls his head to kiss my

thigh where my dress has ridden up. It sends a shiver up my spine, his lips on my skin, and I watch his eyelashes fan across his cheeks. His hand finally leaves my ankle, gliding a few inches up and then stopping to knead the muscle.

He kisses my thigh again.

"What are you doing?" I whisper.

His eyes open, deep and dark but literally twinkling from the reflection of the Christmas lights in his gaze. He turns, rising on a knee to face me.

"You know exactly what I'm doing." One of his hands grips under my thigh and guides my legs to uncross. He's between my knees now, and as far slumped down as I am and as far up my hem has ridden, he might be able to see the dark thong I'm wearing that's soaked through.

He must see it. His gaze is so focused between my legs and it's so intense, I shiver again.

Is he going to go down on me right here in the living room, where anyone could walk in and see us?

He blinks and shifts, rising to lean over me and placing a knee on the seat between my legs. He kisses me firmly, and then pulls back, whispering against my lips, "Come to bed with me."

17

BEA

I NOD AGAINST CHARLIE'S MOUTH, AND IN ONE QUICK SWOOP HE picks me up. I squeak in surprise but he shushes me with his kiss.

After Charlie's freshman year at college, he came home for the summer. I had just moved out of my parents' house and into an apartment with roommates—roommates who didn't hide having sex and had shifts at their jobs that would leave Charlie and me home alone for long stretches. I'd prepared by making a list of everything I wanted to do. One of those things was sex against the wall.

For a myriad of reasons, that didn't work very well. Neither did the shower sex. But now, Charlie's arms feel sturdy, like maybe we could actually pull off that move if we tried it.

Instead, though, Charlie carries me. He navigates around the furniture and up the stairs, and I take advantage of having his neck right in front of me. I lick his pulse point, which causes him to tighten his grip on my ass, squeezing me closer. I nuzzle the skin right below his ear and make my way to his Adam's apple, where I press kisses until he carefully shuts his bedroom door and kneels on the bed, leaning over to gently put me down.

"Brat," he whispers against my lips.

I smile, but he kisses it away.

Between my legs, Charlie is hard and my dress has ridden up to my waist. That soaked thong isn't doing anything to protect me from the grinding motion Charlie is doing with his hips, and it's making me squirm.

Charlie gives my lip a nibble, tugging it gently before he pulls away.

"I have a question for you."

He didn't bother to turn any lights on, but the blinds in his room are open and the Christmas lights on the exterior of the house make it unusually bright.

"Hmm. Is it like a 'should I grab a condom' question or a 'what is the meaning of life' question?"

I feel his stomach bounce with a silent laugh. "It's more of a question about this . . ." His hand snakes up my body and settles on my throat.

Oh.

I swallow and can feel the extra pressure from his grip.

"What do you want to know?" I whisper.

"Did you like this back when we were together before?"

"Maybe. I don't know. You never held me like that."

There's a beat of silence while his thumb strokes the side of my neck. "Other men, though?"

"No."

I can feel how pleased this makes him.

Neanderthal.

"Is it the feeling of being caught? Or do you like breath play?"

"I don't know," I admit. "I didn't realize I liked it until yesterday."

He kisses me, closed mouth against my lips, and then shifts to the side, propping his head up on his other hand while he looks down at me. The hand on my throat keeps stroking.

"I like that I'm learning new things about you."

I tilt my head. "Tell me a new thing about *you*."

He's quiet for a moment, thinking. "I like being bitten."

I click my teeth, earning a laugh.

"Where?"

"My chest, my shoulder. Hickeys optional. Nail scratches too."

He's done that with other women, I realize. Of course he has; I wasn't expecting that he was celibate.

I'm quiet for so long he continues without prompting. "I wish I'd told you back then."

My head rears back in surprise—or at least as far back as it can go when I'm being lightly held against the bed. "You knew back then?"

"Well, I wanted to try it."

I'm flabbergasted. And a little hurt. I'd had a list of things to try, and here was this kink that Charlie had *known* he'd wanted to do.

"Why didn't you ask me?"

His thumb strokes my neck. "I don't know. Maybe I was embarrassed. I would have had to explain . . ." He clears his throat. "I would have had to talk about watching porn halfway across the country from you and about how I missed you *and* sex. I wasn't—I wasn't used to asking for things from you and I just thought I was the luckiest guy. I didn't want to make things harder for either of us. How could I need anything more?"

I look up at Charlie, searching. So much has changed in the eight years since we were together, and while we were each other's firsts in a lot of ways, our relationship wasn't perfect. It was the relationship of two young people navigating growing up and apart.

I let that absorb and resolve to think about it more later. But for right now . . .

Reaching up, I undo the top button on Charlie's oxford. I work my way down, pulling the tail out of his pants, and then run my hands up Charlie's chest. We're kissing again, and I twist us so that Charlie's on his back.

He stretches an arm over his head, watching me with dark eyes, his chest rising and falling in eager anticipation.

"Tell me if I go too hard," I whisper right into his pec before I bite down.

His breath catches and he shifts before murmuring, "Harder."

I do, and he sucks in a hiss, his hips lifting off the bed. Before I can react, he's breaking the connection and reaching down, tugging my dress over my head until I protest and tell him there's a side zipper. Once my dress is off, Charlie flips us and slides his body down mine, kissing and licking as he goes. He digs beneath me to unhook my bra and nips and sucks my nipples until they're stiff and achy.

Charlie runs a finger down my thong and I stifle a groan when the gentle touch runs over my clit.

He takes his mouth off my right breast with a pop. "Do you still prefer fingers over mouth?"

I look at him in the dark. He told me what he wants, and I should be honest with him even if it hurts his pride. He said he's more skilled now, but . . .

"No," I say. "I get off better with oral now."

He comes up and kisses me hard. "Good."

I smile as he moves down, until his fingers push my thong aside and his mouth covers me, and then I gasp.

Charlie is *into* it. He works his tongue over me, tasting me and playing with me, eliciting quiet gasps and twitches. I reach down and grip his hair, tugging him closer and silently begging for him to make me come. He sucks on me hard, rolling my clit between his lips until my thighs clamp around his head and I come in long, glorious waves against his mouth.

18

CHARLIE

Bea quivered—*fucking quivered*—when she came, her feet twitching against my back and her thighs trembling against my ears when she clenched. I'm replaying the feeling over and over again in my mind while she's coming down from her orgasm, and I fucking want to make her do it again.

My dick is so hard through my pants and my lower half is hanging off the edge of the bed, toes digging into the carpet to give me traction. The sheet beneath Bea's ass is damp, as is my face and her thighs. It smells so fucking good.

"Charlie?" Bea murmurs, and I lift my head. "Do I get to ask the condom question now?"

I laugh and press a kiss to her thigh. *Soon*, I promise her pussy, *I'll get to do that again.*

For now, though, I push to my feet and wipe my mouth on the placket of my shirt. "It's in the bathroom. I'll be right back."

She hums, and it takes me a minute to tear away from the sight of Bea blissed out on my bed. I tiptoe across the hallway to the bathroom and dig around in my dopp kit until I find the condoms I have stashed in there.

On my way back across the hall, I hear a noise from downstairs—the unmistakable sound of someone throwing up. I still, listening, until it comes again.

Shit.

I put the condom in my pocket and creep down the stairs. The light's on in the hall bathroom, and pushing the door open reveals Kayla and Jasper, who look up from the bathroom floor. Kayla's hugging the toilet bowl, her hair in a greasy bun, and Jasper sits next to her, rubbing her back.

"Hey," I say.

Jasper grimaces, and Kayla just hangs on to the toilet.

"Did we wake you?" he asks.

I shake my head and crouch down to their level. "I was still up. You need anything?"

Kayla spits into the toilet. "No." She sounds miserable, and I feel for her.

"I guess morning sickness is a misnomer?"

Kayla gasps and whips her head to glare at Jasper. "You *told him*?"

"He guessed!" Jasper says defensively.

"We're not supposed to tell anyone yet! And I—" Kayla cuts herself off, her eyes on my chest. Her gaze narrows. "Is that . . . is that a bite mark?"

I look down. My shirt has gaped open since I never buttoned it back up. I pull one side closed to cover up the red teeth marks.

Kayla glares at me. "So help me god if that was from anyone's teeth but Bea's—"

"It was Bea," I say quickly. "I swear."

Kayla relaxes, and then tenses again. "Okay, well don't take this as commentary on that but—*blerghghghghghgh*."

Unholy noises come out of Kayla as she barfs. Jasper grimaces—or never stopped grimacing since I got here—and rubs her back more.

I'm not sure how to get myself out of this politely, so I wait. Kayla has nothing left in her stomach to toss up, so it doesn't take long until she's spitting, flushing, and Jasper's wiping her face with a piece of toilet paper.

"Just go," she says miserably, and I do. I retreat up the stairs, condom burning a hole in my pocket, only to open the door to my room and see Bea sprawled out on my bed, asleep.

19

BEA

I WAKE UP HUGGING A FURNACE. IT'S SO HOT UNDER THE COVER, I might even be sweating.

I open my eyes and see the broad expanse of a back—Charlie's back. I'm jet-packing him, my arms around his waist, his ass in my groin, and my thighs against the back of his.

Oh yes. Charlie went down on me last night and it was so fucking hot. If I were a camp counselor, Charlie would receive the Most Improved award for his oral skills.

My forehead rests against his upper back, and his muscles move slightly—he's awake.

"Morning," I say.

Charlie stretches away from me and I hear the *thunk* of his phone hitting the nightstand before he turns around to face me. Charlie's shirtless—yum—and I spot a flash of black fabric and bare legs under the covers. He's wearing boxer briefs, and I'm naked.

I sit bolt upright. "Oh my god, did I fall asleep while having sex with you?"

The bed shakes with Charlie's laughter. I try to smack his

shoulder with the back of my hand, but he grabs it instead and pulls me down.

"You fell asleep before that could get started. Your post-orgasm bliss was too strong and you were out by the time I got back here."

I groan. "You're going to be insufferable today, aren't you?"

Before Charlie can answer, there's a knock on the door. We both sit up and I clutch the sheet to my boobs. "Yeah?" Charlie calls softly.

Naomi's voice comes through the door. "Bea? You may want to sneak out before anyone else wakes up."

Whelp. One sister knows where I spent the night, although I don't know how I thought I was going to get around that. "Shit, yeah." I throw off the covers and search for my dress. I find it haphazardly draped over Charlie's open luggage and grab my thong and bra from their similar scattered fate.

"Hey," Charlie says softly, and I pause. He's stood up from the bed, and I get to see Charlie in all his grown-up glory.

When I finally meet his eyes, his gaze is soft and warm as he pulls me in for a kiss.

I deepen it and cling to him. Neither of us are minty-fresh, but Charlie tastes like Charlie, and I like it.

He finally pulls away. "Go shower. We'll talk later."

———

By the time I shower and go downstairs, the entire house is up except for Kayla. Jasper is in the kitchen making pancakes while the moms are at the kitchen counter with Gary. My dad and the rest of the kids are at the table.

"Grab a plate, Bea," Jasper calls. There's a stack on the counter, so I grab one and sidle up next to him. A large hot griddle and two pans on the stove are cranking out steaming pancakes. He gives me an odd look, and even though I showered I feel like I have a "freshly orgasmed" stamp on my face. He gestures to a pancake. "This one's about ready to flip. Want anything on it?" He nods to bowls of various sizes filled with nuts and chocolate chips and fruit.

I grab a handful of chocolate chips and sprinkle them on the pancake, followed by walnuts. He flips it, and I wait.

Across the kitchen, Charlie's gaze catches mine. He's facing me, drinking from a mug. He hasn't showered, I don't think, and when he lowers his coffee, my eyes snag on his mouth.

"Hey Bea," Dad says over his shoulder. He's sitting across from Charlie, facing away from me.

"Morning, Dad."

"Know why they call them pancakes?"

I brace myself for a dad joke. "No. Why?"

"'Cause they're cakes made in a pan, duh."

Charlie chokes on his coffee and Jasper chuckles next to me.

I put my hands on my hips, plate against my thigh. "What, no dad joke? I'm totally disappointed in you."

"That was a dad joke!" he insists.

"That was, like, the opposite of a dad joke."

Dad half turns in his chair. "Fine, you want a dad joke? Why was the pancake arrested?"

Oh no, what have I done?

"Psst." Jasper has my pancake on his spatula.

I hold out my plate and begrudgingly ask, "Why, Dad?"

"Unwaffle activities."

I can't help but grin, and while the rest of the table groans or chuckles, I walk over and take the empty chair next to Lance. "Morning, everyone," I say, purposefully not looking at Charlie.

Unfortunately this means I'm looking directly across the

table at my roomie who knows that I didn't come to bed last night.

She smirks at me. "Good morning, Bea," she calls in a singsong voice. "I slept *so well* last night. How did you sleep?"

———

DAD AND GARY ARE THE ONLY TWO WHO WANT TO SKI TODAY, SO they go off to the resort together. Kayla finally wakes up and Jasper whips up more pancakes for her. Mom asks if anyone wants to go for a walk with her. We all say no, and she goes by herself. Susan pulls out an approximately nine-thousand-piece puzzle, and my sisters and I spend the morning fighting over edge pieces and puzzle strategy while Charlie has his laptop out on the kitchen counter.

I glance over at him a lot, unable to help myself. It shouldn't bother me that he's not taking part in the puzzle—everyone's allowed to do their own thing. We don't have to be together 24/7. After all, Jasper's playing games on his phone on the couch, and Lance has disappeared to who-knows-where. Probably the bedroom to take some time to recharge his introverted batteries away from my loud, obnoxious family.

Charlie is probably working. But maybe he's looking at customer data and advertising reports.

A thought occurs to me—what if he doesn't know the data is being abused?

Finally, I give in. "What are you doing over there?"

He sighs and rubs his face. "Emails, mostly. Also, boring stuff." He smiles.

"What kind of boring stuff?" Yvette asks from where she's leaning over the puzzle, trying to figure out which blue ocean edge piece is the right blue ocean edge piece out of probably a hundred.

"Someone released a paper on argument mining last month and I'm just now getting around to reading it."

Argument mining? What the hell does that mean?

"You know, the holidays are supposed to be time off," Kayla teases.

"Tell that to the fifty-seven *important* emails that have come into my inbox this morning."

Once again, I'm thankful that Nash takes the holidays off and insists that Heartly's offices operate with minimal staff. While I still check my email and Nash's every day, a few responses are all that's required.

There's a knock at the door, and we all look at one another.

"Are you expecting anyone?" Mom asks the room, and we all shake our heads. Charlie catches my gaze, and I can see the thought behind his eyes: *Is that Kit again?*

I shrug while Yvette gets up to go to the door.

She returns a few minutes later with a package. "It's for Bea!" she announces in a singsong voice.

I sit up and she deposits the box in my lap. It's fairly big, wide enough that Kayla has to scootch over, but thin. And it is definitely addressed to me.

"Who's it from?" Kayla asks.

The return address is my office. Huh. Usually Nash gives me a gift card for Christmas plus a generous bonus. I'm not sure what this could be.

"Open it," Yvette squeals. She *loves* presents, and any kind of surprise, really.

I contemplate waiting till Christmas to open it for about two seconds, and then I rip into the box. Inside, there's a smaller silver box—similar dimensions, just smaller—nestled in tissue paper with a card on top. The card partially covers the label, but I already know the brand: Balenciaga.

I open the card.

. . .

Bea,

I hope you have a great Christmas with your family. You're the best assistant I've ever had. Thank you for your support and insight throughout the year.

Nash

Bea,

We are long overdue for a night out. I know just the place. Let's put it on the calendar when you get back!

XO,

Clara

With the note card are two gift cards—one to YSL Beauty, my favorite makeup store, the other a Visa prepaid card.

Yvette snatches the Visa card. "Oh, how much do you think is on it?"

I ignore her and lift the smaller box up. I carefully open it. Inside is neatly folded wool and lace and when I stand and hold it out to full length, I recognize it.

The last time I saw this skirt was two or three months ago. Clara had borrowed one of Heartly's conference rooms to have a meeting with a woman who was wearing it, and I complimented it. I didn't even know that Clara had overheard, much less remembered.

It's fitted and just my size. It falls to just below my knee and reveals an underskirt of matching black lace.

It's so pretty it takes my breath away, but is not so extravagant that I can't wear it to work.

I also know that it costs two grand. It's a very generous gift.

Mom takes it from me. "This is beautiful. It will look so lovely on you."

Kayla lifts the outer layer to see how far the lace goes and how it's attached, which makes us laugh. Yvette holds it up to her hips. "If only I lived closer to you. We could share wardrobes."

Naomi snorts. "Like she wants to wear your Southwest uniform."

"At least we don't have to wear neckerchiefs anymore."

I ignore my sisters and take the gift upstairs to my room, and when I get back, everyone's returned their attention to the puzzle.

The dads return home hungry, and we all have to eat in the living room so as not to disturb the puzzle on the dining room table. Afterward, we grab pillows and blankets and watch Christmas movies in the basement. Me, Charlie, Yvette, Lance, and Naomi all lie on the floor while our parents are on the couch and Kayla and Jasper share the love seat on the side.

Charlie holds my hand under a thick fleece blanket.

After Hans Gruber plunges to his death, we disperse. Kayla goes to take a nap, Lance stays downstairs by himself, and the rest of us converge in the kitchen.

"What are you cooking?" Mom asks while pouring herself a glass of wine. Tonight, dinner is up to me, Charlie, and Naomi, the three poor unattached souls teamed up like the singles table at a wedding.

"Pork tenderloin," Naomi says.

"Oh, are you roasting?" Jaspers asks from his perch on one of the counter stools. Knowing him, he'll probably stay there and watch us cook all evening.

"Yup. With potatoes, apples, and butternut squash," Naomi replies.

"Mom," Charlie says from where he's pulling the marinated meat out of the fridge. "Do you want me to light the firepit outside?"

"Oh!" Susan brightens. "What a lovely idea. And I've got

some juniper berries and cedar branches I foraged this morning. I would love to make an offering. But your dad can do the fire."

Gary grunts. "Do we have enough wood?"

I struggle to hold in my laughter.

"Plenty of wood," Charlie says mildly.

When our parents have retreated to the backyard, it's just the four of us. I begin chopping the apples. "Do you think that's a good size, Jasper?"

He leans over and inspects my work. Then he fixes my grip on the knife. "Lord, did you forget *everything* I've taught you?"

"I don't cook in the city and you wouldn't either."

Jasper harrumphs and sits back down, sipping his beer. Behind me, there's a cacophony of noises and a "whoops" from Charlie as he digs through the cabinets in the butler's pantry on the other side of the kitchen.

"You okay back there?" Jasper calls.

"Maybe. Um, which pan do you think I should use?"

Jasper puts on a big show of sighing and getting up to help Charlie. Naomi, who's next to me peeling the squash, and I share an amused look.

She takes a step closer. "So, what happened last night?"

I make a face and she makes one right back. "Not like that! But, are y'all back together now?"

"I don't know," I whisper. "We didn't talk about it."

Behind me, Charlie and Jasper have dropped their voices too, and I can't hear them over the sizzle of the pork browning.

"He's in your city now," she continues.

"I know. But he works a lot."

She points her seed-scraper spoon at me. "Pot. Kettle."

I roll my eyes. My family loves to think of me as a workaholic. The reality is that my job would have a great work-life balance if I had a personal life. But if there's nothing but shitty dates and a quiet apartment waiting for me, why shouldn't I put so much time and effort into my job?

"Okay. Well, maybe you both being workaholics is a good thing. I mean, imagine your life in New York with a boyfriend. Wouldn't it be ideal if he understood the pressures of a job and had his own to keep him busy?"

We both let that sit for a minute. Maybe Naomi is expecting me to be picturing coming home from a long day of work just in time to get in bed with Charlie and catch each other up on our days. Or us sitting together with our work calendars and negotiating whose office events we make an appearance at and whose we skip.

But that's not what I have in mind. Those fantasies I have about a charming small-town man and love at first sight? At the end of those fantasies, it's obvious what happens—I quit my job and leave the city.

I want to love to spend time with someone. I want to do things with them, and I don't know what I would do for work if I quit Heartly—it is a great job, after all—but I want Heartly to be the second thing I think about when I wake up in the morning. Not the first.

I glance behind me at Charlie. He and Jasper are putting the tenderloin on a roasting rack and I'm falling behind on chopping the produce.

A week ago, I could have sworn that Charlie thought about work first thing in the morning. But there was that morning a few days ago when he was trying to get me back in bed before he fully woke up. And yet, this morning, he was on his phone. Probably working.

I sigh.

While none of the small-town hunks I've met so far have made my heart skip a beat, I've fallen right back into bed with the big-city man who's more likely to break my heart again than give me a happily-ever-after.

20

CHARLIE

Jasper and I get the pork in the pan and bring it over to where Bea and Naomi are chopping the vegetables. And by "Jasper and I," I mean he put the pork on the pan while peppering me with questions about last night.

Not asking for details . . . just more like "what the fuck is going on?" questions.

"What have y'all been talking about?" Naomi asks us, a smug look on her face. Bea elbows her.

"Oh, you know, this and that," Jasper says, equally smug. "And you?"

Okay, so they both know that Bea and I hooked up. But they don't know that the other knows.

And Bea doesn't know that Jasper knows.

Oy vey.

"Just a sisterly chat." Naomi winks at me.

"Sisterly chat," Jasper echoes. "And our manly men talk."

Manly men. I run a hand down my face.

When I can see again, Naomi and Jasper are glaring at each other.

"What were you two talking about?" she demands.

"Nothing I can tell you," he counters.

"I bet it was boring," Naomi says.

A headache is building. I know Jasper and Naomi love each other, but they bicker like siblings. Bea rubs her temples.

"Are you two actually fighting over *our* secret?" I ask.

They both gasp and speak at the same time.

"He knows?"

"She knows?"

Followed quickly by Bea's, "Jasper knows?"

"Y'all." I press my palms together, begging. "Be cool, okay?"

"When did Jasper find out?" Bea asks.

"You were asleep."

The back door opens and Mom flounces in. The four of us break apart like billiard balls. "Helloooo!" She raises an empty glass. "Out of wine. I think I'll just grab a whole bottle. Charlie, the firepit was a wonderful idea." Mom brushes past me, smelling of smoke with a hint of tannins, and opens the fridge. "How's it going in here?"

"Fine," the four of us say in unison.

The fridge door falls closed and Mom peers at the pan. The tenderloin stands alone, the rest of the meal in various stages of preparedness. "What time do you think we'll eat?"

Jasper glances at the fridge and does math. "A little late. Sorry. I have untrained sous chefs, you know."

"You're the sous chef," Naomi grumbles.

Mom kisses her cheek. "Better grab some snacks, then." She reopens the fridge and roots around, bottle of wine under her arm, until she finds the hummus. She swipes a box of crackers off the counter on her way out. "Shout when it's ready!"

The three of us vote Jasper off the island and banish him back to the stool. We focus on getting the job done, and soon the tenderloin and accouterments are in the oven. Then we turn to the stove to make six side dishes.

God it takes a lot of food to feed eleven people.

Somehow, between stirring pots and washing dishes, Bea and I have a few minutes alone. And I'm not risking tonight.

I sidle up behind Bea at the stove and kiss the back of her neck. Her inhale is sharp and surprised.

"Come to bed with me tonight."

She pauses, the spoon she was stirring with still halfway in the simmering water. "Charlie . . ."

She doesn't finish the thought, but her tone makes me think it wasn't going to be *yes, Charlie, I'll come to your bed and we can give each other orgasms all night long.*

Instead I kiss lower, trailing my lips down to her shoulder and nipping gently. She leans against me and I grip her hips with my hands.

"Let me make you feel good," I whisper. "Let me show you how amazing we are together."

She laughs, but it's almost more of an exhale than humor. "I *remember* how good we were together."

I press my nose into the soft space under her ear. "No. You remember how good we *were*. Let me show you how good we *are*."

Right now, I don't have enough money or time. But it's so close I can taste it, and I will do whatever I can if Bea would give me another chance. It's a miracle that I'm standing in this kitchen with her and she's thinking about it.

Footsteps approach, and Bea glances at me over her shoulder as I step away. "Okay," she says, just as Jasper comes around the corner.

―――――

After dinner, we pick another movie—*How the Grinch Stole Christmas*—and resume our places in the basement. Just as Jim Carrey accepts his position as Holiday Cheermeister, Arlo calls.

Perfect timing. I excuse myself and retreat upstairs.

I spend fifteen minutes on the phone, catching up with him and dillydallying until, maybe, no one will notice I don't come back.

The movie's still playing when I hang up with him, but I don't go back downstairs. I climb up to my room instead, and when I open the door, Bea is lying on my bed.

My heart blooms.

The lamp on the bedside is on and she's still dressed.

I smile at her, close the door behind me, and crawl up her body. Bea smiles back, those two dimples deepening. I put my hands on either side of her face, stroke her cheeks with my thumbs.

"Hi," she whispers.

"Hey," I say. "Done grinching around downstairs?"

She laughs and I kiss her. It's slow and sweet, and I lay my body over hers.

I move my lips down her face, kissing a dimple before nipping down her neck. Bea runs her hands through my hair, pressing my face further into her skin.

Piece by piece, we undress each other. Under her sweatshirt is a tank top, and then a cotton bra that I pull over her head. Bea runs her hands over my chest, exploring my chest hair, pinches a nipple, and touches the tips of her fingers to where she bit me yesterday. The mark is still there, just light bruising with no broken skin.

Perfect.

I roll to the side and Bea follows. I kiss her slowly, running the back of my hands over her breasts and belly. Her areolas are so pale, I wouldn't be able to tell where they start except that the skin gets even softer around her nipples. I stroke them with my thumb while Bea moans, breaking our kiss.

Bea gets louder and she whines. I reward her by reaching down into her pajama pants and panties, and finding her clit with my fingers.

"Charlie," Bea snaps and grabs my wrist.

"What?" I tease her, the words against her lips.

"Can you please fuck me now?"

"I have to make sure you're ready for me." My fingers twitch, just barely brushing her clit.

"I'm ready," she insists. "Charlie, I want you."

"Prove it. Let go."

She releases my wrist, and I press two fingers against her clit and slide them down and into her pussy. She gasps and squirms. I pump my hand and circle her clit with my thumb.

"Fuck, fuck, fuck, fuck," she whispers.

"So good. You're so beautiful like this."

"Charlie. Charlie," she chants. "Oh god."

"It's going to be so good, isn't it? I'm going to make you come, and then I'm going to fuck you all night. I'm going to take care of you, give you everything you need."

Her eyes meet mine, half-lidded and sex-drugged. "Charlie. Can you . . . can you hold my throat?"

Fuck yes. I shift up, keeping my fingers inside her but sitting up enough to get my weight off my arm. My knees straddle one of her legs, and my hand is still pumping into her.

"Tap me twice to stop, okay? I'm going to be gentle though."

She nods, and I set my hand on her throat, my thumb just at her pulse point and my fingers wrapped around the other side. I'm not applying much pressure, just enough so she can feel me.

So that she's pinned beneath me.

She looks up at me, complete trust in her eyes. I would never hurt her, I would do anything for her, and that will never change.

This is what it's like to love someone for most of your life.

I can feel her getting close.

"I've got you, beautiful," I tell her. "Come for me."

Bea comes, back bowing and her throat pressing up

against my hand. Her body clenches around my fingers but I keep pumping, telling her how gorgeous she is and how good she feels.

After a few shudders, her whole body goes bowstring tight again, her pussy fluttering. Her eyes roll back and she bites her lip, hard. I can't wait for those teeth to be biting down on me.

God, it feels like a dream to be here.

Finally, Bea twists away from me. "Okay, okay." There's laughter in her voice, and I carefully slip my fingers out and let her throat go.

Bea breathes hard for a few moments, her rib cage rising and falling, before she rolls her head over to look at me. She reaches down to where I'm still straddling her and grips my hard cock beneath my boxer briefs.

"Please."

21

BEA

I'M HAVING SERIOUS FLASHBACKS TO MY TEENAGE YEARS. MY parents are in the house, Charlie's scrambling to undress, and I lie on the bed watching him roll a condom on.

The differences are that I've just had the most intense orgasm of my life and that we're all grown up.

Charlie climbs back onto the bed, lining himself up with me. His forearms rest on either side of my head, his fingers tangling in my hair. He presses a sweet kiss to my lips.

"Ready?" he asks.

I grab his arms, my fingers sinking into his biceps, which strain from holding himself up. I hitch a leg up over his hip and I can feel him right at my entrance.

"Yeah," I whisper, and he eases in. His dark eyelashes flutter in pleasure and my head tilts back, my mouth falling open as he slides all the way in.

"Oh, Bea . . ."

Charlie kisses my dimple. He kisses his way down my neck, his warm breath tickling my skin. The fullness of him becomes unbearable, and I need him to move.

He does, and it's a long slow drag in and out. And another. Then another.

My heel digs into his ass to spur him on, but he ignores me. These slow, steady strokes border on torture. I'm still holding on to his biceps, and they flex beneath my fingers.

I squeeze, and then shift to dig my nails in.

Charlie grunts.

He shifts slightly so he isn't going as deep inside me, but his cockhead is rubbing just the right places inside me. His tempo picks up too, and I squeeze my eyes shut.

He groans over me and then lowers his mouth to my ear and whispers, "Is this new too? Can you come on my dick?"

I don't know. It's rare for me, but the pressure is building, and it helps that I've already come hard on his fingers. Sweat blooms over Charlie's skin and the muscles of his jaw shift against mine as he clenches his teeth. His chest brushes against mine with every pump of his hips, pressing our bodies closer together.

My core winds so tight it aches.

"I've got you, beautiful. I'm here. You can let go."

I'm so close. Charlie keeps talking to me, low murmured whispers that take on a desperate tone. He feels so good, and as the pressure builds, I put my mouth on his shoulder, the meaty part, to muffle myself. I'm still not sure if I can . . .

My orgasm rips through me. With Charlie's body pinning me down, I have nowhere to go and I bite back a scream.

Literally. My teeth dig into Charlie's muscle as my pussy clenches around him. Charlie's fingers tighten in my hair and he slams into me. I'm still coming and Charlie's telling me to bite him harder and I do and he hisses and fucks into me. He was holding himself back before, and now he's wild.

With one last thrust, he stays embedded in me. I'm still in aftershocks, but I can feel his cock twitching as he pulses into the condom.

And then it's all heavy breathing and loose muscles and a deep, sinking relaxation.

I let go with my teeth, sucking slightly as I pull away, and he shudders.

"Fuck," he says into my hair.

I let go of his biceps too, and run my hands down his broad back, enjoying the shift of muscle and the feel of his sweat-slicked skin.

Charlie pulls back and removes his fingers from my scalp. He smooths my hair away from my face and presses light kisses over my cheeks and chin.

We're quiet for a long time, just soft kisses and stroking hands, until Charlie's chest bounces with a chuckle.

"God damn," he says, still breathless. "Beautiful, I always knew you'd ruined my heart, and now you've ruined my cock."

———

I WAKE CHARLIE UP BY CURLING MY TONGUE AROUND HIS COCK and get a thrill when my name is the first thing he says. When he gets close, I dig my nails into his thighs and swallow him deep as he comes.

When he tries to pull me up the bed, I shy away.

"Bathroom," I whisper, and I throw my pajamas on before sneaking out the door. I don't know what time it is, but the house is quiet and there's gray light coming through the bathroom window.

When I finish rinsing with mouthwash and peeing, I open the door and jolt when I see Naomi standing in the hallway.

"Pajama delivery," she says, and hands me a package.

Ah, right. It's Christmas Eve, and it's pajama day. The stack of soft cotton in my hand is bright red with . . . yes, that's little reindeer leaping around on the fabric. There are two pairs and . . . oh no. This year, they're onesies.

"Naomi—" I start with a half whine, half laugh, but she throws up her hands.

"You know I didn't pick them out!"

She huffs back to our room and I go back to Charlie's. He's sitting up in bed on his phone, but he puts it down as I close the door behind me.

I keep my hands and the pajamas behind my back. "Special delivery."

He raises an eyebrow. "Is that what we're calling it now?"

I laugh and he throws his legs out of bed, stalking toward me. He cups both of his hands on either side of my head and smooths my hair back.

"God, you're beautiful."

I saw myself in the mirror, of course. My hair's in a messy bun, tufts sticking up haphazardly and darker hair poking up in bumps through the lighter blond. My face is bare, and without any eye makeup, I always look half-asleep.

I let the pajamas fall from my hands as Charlie pushes me against the door, his tongue in my mouth and his hands tilting my head back. He's put pajama bottoms on, but his chest is bare, and I run my hands up the ripples of muscles on his sides. His body curves against mine, and he breaks his mouth away to kiss my neck, and he drops to his knees—

Bang, bang, bang.

The door behind us shudders, and I jolt.

"We're waiting for you," Yvette yells through the door.

Charlie's head presses into my stomach, and we both shake with laughter. When my heart stops racing, Charlie sits back on his heels and looks up at me. "Later," he suggests.

"Later," I agree, and while Charlie goes to the bathroom, I put my onesie reindeer pajamas on and head downstairs.

22

CHARLIE

A FEW YEARS AGO, JODY AND ERIK LAMENTED THAT THEY ONLY got all their kids together over the holidays, since the younger generation lived all over the country. At the time, there weren't weddings and babies on the horizon, so Jody suggested we take a family picture during the Christmas week.

Hence, the themed pajamas.

I zip my onesie and flip the hood up. Yes, there's a hood with felt antlers on it. The onesie has pockets but doesn't have booties, so I put my phone into the pocket, step into my slippers, and head downstairs.

"Are you whistling?" Yvette asks. She's seated at the kitchen counter next to Lance. Jody and Erik were in charge of breakfast this morning, and the cloyingly sweet smell of cinnamon rolls and icing hangs in the air.

Lance tips his chin up to me in greeting as I grab a plate. Bea's not down yet, so I grab a plate for her too and give her the gooiest middle piece out of the pan.

Yvette raises an eyebrow and opens her mouth, but Lance nudges her before she can say anything.

Saved by the peacemaker. I put a fresh pod into the coffee machine and wait for it to brew.

Yvette sighs and rolls her head onto Lance's shoulder. "If you don't want me to razz him, you could at least get me another cinnamon roll."

Lance smiles and reaches down the kitchen island for another pastry. Yvette sighs happily and kisses his shoulder before she digs in.

The rest of the family is at the table, Jasper and Erik deep in conversation and I hear the words *carrot* and *powder,* so who knows what they are talking about. Naomi's talking to Mom and Kayla. Everyone's wearing their onesies and half the hoods are up.

I look back at Lance and Yvette. She feeds him a bite of cinnamon roll and leans against him. Next year, they'll be married. Right now, they've got their wedding to look forward to.

This could be me and Bea next year. Sitting by ourselves, on the cusp of the rest of our lives together.

Movement catches my eye and I notice Bea enter the room about two seconds before everyone else does.

"Good morning, sleepyhead," Erik calls.

Bea has brushed her hair, and it's gathered at the nape in a smooth bun. She's still bare-faced, and those dimples pop, first for her dad, and then even deeper when she sees me.

"Oh god, y'all are insufferable." Yvette rolls her eyes and Lance blushes in secondhand embarrassment.

"I'm sorry, didn't you just swoon over your fiancé getting you a cinnamon roll?" I stick out my tongue at her. "Talk about insufferable."

Yvette laughs and Lance blushes harder.

Bea joins us in the kitchen, and I hand her the plate and coffee. She accepts it and her gaze drops to my lips like she's thinking about kissing me good morning in front of God and everyone.

She doesn't though. Instead she turns and takes a seat at the table.

"Insufferable," Yvette mouths to me while I start a second cup of coffee.

By the time I sit down, almost everyone has finished eating, so I enjoy my cinnamon rolls in silence, listening to the chatter about the day's plans. First there are the family photos by the fireplace—Jody has made a list; everyone being serious, everyone being goofy, the Cummingses, the Cummingses plus in-laws, the Dunskys, and every individual couple. Bea and I aren't on the list, and I look up at her, trying to catch her eye and gauge her thoughts.

We should have talked about this last night, but I was too sex-drunk to have a scary conversation. What happens next? What do we do when we get back to the city?

Bea doesn't look at me though, she's too busy plotting something with Jasper—ah, a snowman-building competition, to be voted on by the moms.

"What is that?" Erik's voice carries over all the other conversations. He's sitting across from me and staring over my left shoulder. The rest of the conversation in the room dips.

I look over my shoulder. Yvette and Lance look at me wide-eyed from the kitchen counter, and then glance behind themselves.

"What?" I ask, before turning back to Erik.

"That." He points and then gets up to reach across the table and flick the hoodie off my head. "Is that a hickey?"

I'm not wearing a shirt underneath the onesie, and I reach up to feel my shoulder. Yes, at the crook of my neck is a tender spot where Bea sunk her teeth last night.

Someone whoops—Jasper, probably, finally able to let out his excitement in public—and across the table Bea buries her blushing face in her hands amid a cacophony of voices.

Mom gets up, then sits down, then gets up again. "Are you two—oh, bless the fates!"

There's a lot of laughter and "finally" and my mom looking like I hung the moon, with tears in her eyes. Just when I think everyone's calming down, Erik speaks up again.

"You better hurry with the grandkids, so Jasper or Kayla junior has someone to play with."

"Dad!" Kayla shouts, and Jasper groans.

"What?" Jody screeches.

Now we're all on our feet, and Kayla's crying and getting tons of hugs.

"We're not out of the first trimester yet. Don't get too excited," Kayla begs, but it mostly falls on deaf ears.

When things finally die down, Jody turns to her husband and backhands him on his shoulder. It's playful . . . kind of.

"You know you're supposed to let a couple announce their own pregnancy!" she scolds him. "How did you even know?" She whacks him again, and he raises his arms in self-defense.

"She's been throwing up all the time. How did you not notice?"

Jody switches to wagging her finger at him viciously. "I need to get you a book on how to be a grandparent. My god."

She dives into a lecture, finger still wagging, and Erik has the decency to look ashamed. In my pocket, my phone buzzes.

I slide it out and see Arlo's name on the screen. It's Christmas Eve, so he's probably calling to wish me a Merry Christmas one last time. I swipe my thumb across the screen and step away from the family and into the butler's pantry. "Good morning," I say.

"Charlie, we have a problem."

23

BEA

It takes me a minute to realize Charlie's not in the room anymore. I look around and spot him in the butler's pantry. He's on the phone, onesie hood down and leaning against the counter. There's a crease between his eyebrows that I watch deepen as the seconds tick by.

His mouth tightens. His fingers grip the phone so tightly they go white. Whoever he's on the phone with is still talking, and Charlie's shrinking with every word into someone that I barely recognize.

My stomach drops.

"Fuck," he says, so quietly that I read his lips more than I hear the words. "Fuck."

This time, the rest of the room hears him and goes quiet.

Charlie turns his back to us and walks away. An uneasy feeling passes over me, and my dad gives me a concerned look.

"Well, let's get the kitchen cleaned up," Mom says, "and when Charlie comes down, we can get started on pictures."

With all of us working together, the leftover cinnamon rolls get packed away and the plates and cutlery go into the dishwasher. Dad gets his tripod and camera set up facing the gorgeous Christmas tree in the front room, and Charlie still hasn't reappeared.

The uneasy feeling has turned into a ball of molten lead in my stomach. It's Christmas Eve, and I remind myself that we've been in our own little bubble in a small town and that the outside world exists. We have jobs that sometimes can't wait and in a parallel universe, my boss would have called me with some crisis.

When Charlie's feet finally tread the stairs coming down, I'm leaning against the couch, arms crossed and half listening to Yvette and Mom talk. I look up and the molten lead freezes.

Charlie's dressed in jeans and boots, and I see the suitcase he's carrying down the stairs before I can see his face.

"I have to go," he says.

Susan gasps. "Charlie. Really?"

"Yes." His voice is a quiet cut, and then he clears his throat and says with more softness this time. "Yes. I'm sorry. Something's come up and I need to get back to the city."

He's not looking at me, but it feels like the gaze of every other person in the room is on me.

"Charlie." This voice is so harsh I barely recognize it. My dad. My affable, jokester dad is *furious*. "This isn't right, Charlie."

"I'm sorry," Charlie repeats, and it's wooden, nothing like the warmth in his voice, his gaze, his hands this morning. He swallows hard and finally looks at me. "Bea, can I borrow your rental car? I'll pay for a driver to get you back to the city."

The room is dead silent. The weight inside me pulls like a chain hanging down into a never-ending pit. And then someone takes my left hand.

It's Lance, sitting on the couch. My quiet, sweet, soon-to-be brother-in-law, the newest member of our family, has taken my hand.

He gets it.

And Charlie never has.

"You don't *have* to go. You're *choosing* to go." My voice is rising, like I'm having an out-of-body experience, like I'm falling right back into the past, where I'm not worth Charlie's attention.

And for a moment, I see emotion cross his face—a flicker of something. Pain? Anguish? Everything softens, and my stupid little heart feels light as air for a moment. It's just long enough that I think, *No, of course not, this time is different. We're all grown up now.*

But then Charlie's face hardens again. "Bea," Charlie says, his voice cracking, as if the emotions that were suppressed have to get out some way and they'll take any path they can get. "Please."

I squeeze Lance's hand and force myself to move. "Fine."

Everyone knows this is anything but fine. I feel immensely stupid, and the looks of pity I'm getting from the rest of the room make me feel about two feet tall.

I let go of Lance's grip and walk to the entryway. Next to the stairwell, there's a shallow bowl where we've taken to keeping our keys so that anyone can shuffle the cars around and get out when they want to. I find the clicker, with its green rental-car tag, and drop it into Charlie's waiting hand.

"I thought this time was different, Charlie."

And I just keep walking. Past Charlie, who flinches and avoids my gaze. I'm an apparition floating by, up the stairs in my reindeer onesie and into the silence of the hallway.

———

HALF AN HOUR LATER, MY PHONE RINGS. I'M LYING ON MY BUNK bed, staring up at the ceiling, and don't even glance at the screen before I answer it. It's Nash's ringtone.

"Hello."

"Bea, how's your Christmas going?"

I stare up at the wooden bed frame. Something's broken inside me. I haven't cried. I guess I haven't been up here long enough for my family to send a delegation (probably Mom), so I've been completely alone.

"Fine," I say.

There's a pause, and when Nash's voice returns, it comes back skeptical. "You don't sound fine. I'm sorry, I shouldn't have called. But is everything okay?"

"It's personal."

Nash snorts. "I think we passed personal a while ago, Bea. After all, you got me through the Great Food Poisoning Incident of 2023 and helped me woo Clara."

I laugh. "I know. And you went out and bought tampons for me in Taiwan. I guess that makes us friends."

"Definitely," he returns without missing a beat. There's a muffled shout. "Clara says she's your friend too, whether you want her or not. I guess we are a package deal," he says, teasingly apologetic. More shouting, and then Nash chuckles. "And everyone else here says Merry Christmas. Now, can you tell me what's going on?"

I sigh. I was expecting one of my sisters or my mom to come up, but the universe sends me Nash? "You remember my ex, the founder of Rivrse?"

There's a pause. "Yeaahhhh . . . he's the reason I'm calling you."

My eyebrows draw together. "What?"

"I take it you didn't see the article yet?"

I sit up and immediately whack my head on the bunk bed and yelp. "Ow. Fuck."

"Bea, you okay?"

I aggressively rub my forehead and give my brain a minute to stop reverberating. "Yes, I'm fine. What article?"

"I'll forward it to you. Read it and call me back, okay?"

We hang up and a few seconds later my phone pings with

a link. It's an article in *The Wall Street Journal* titled "How These Virtual Reality Headsets Are Using Your Data—and Why You Need FTC Protection More Than Ever."

I click the link and read. By the time I'm finished, my hands are shaking. I call Nash back.

"Did you read it?"

"Yes. So our advertising team was right."

"Yup. This journalist was months ahead of us. If he's right, either ImmUniverse or Rivrse is in a breach of terms of service not just with us but with Facebook, Google, any other advertising platform they've been using. There's going to be an investigation and probably lawsuits. ImmUniverse's stock value dropped fifteen percent today. This is huge."

"Oh my god."

"Bea," Nash starts gently. "ImmUniverse might be big enough to get out of this in one piece because they're one of the biggest VR manufacturers and they have a massive amount of resources. Rivrse is . . ."

"Oh my god," I say again. "Rivrse is done for."

24

CHARLIE

YEARS AGO, I LEARNED ABOUT GLACIAL ERRATIC BOULDERS. These rocks would embed into glaciers that would carry them away from their source. Then the glaciers would melt and deposit the rocks in weird locations.

Sometimes, the melt would get caught by an ice dam, and the water would build up, piling debris until the dam broke, launching a cataclysmic flood across the lands and sending the rocks even further at up to eighty miles per hour.

That's what I feel like right now. The dam has broken and I've been swept up and somehow deposited on the highway headed toward the city at nearly the same speed.

I should be thinking about the call with Arlo—who said, "I strongly recommend we back out of this agreement and hire a legal team"—and the article he had sent me—". . . grossly misusing customer data for no less than spying on their customers . . ."

Instead, I see Bea.

I don't want to think about that look on her face. I don't want to hear the anger in her dad's voice or see the way Lance grabbed her hand in a comforting touch.

But now that I'm in the flow of traffic and the panic is

receding into mind-numbing automation—turn signal on, check mirrors, change lanes—I can't stop picturing it.

What have I done?

I can fix this. One thing at a time. I'll get to the city and I'll —I'll . . .

What, exactly?

Arlo said he was going to call me back after he spoke to a lawyer. He suggested I call my marketing manager, Tasha, who's probably down in San Diego with her family right now. I need to touch base with my staff—probably my entire company. If they haven't seen the article by now, they will soon.

But none of that is going to solve the problem.

A car honks and I realize I've slowed down on the highway. I push the gas pedal to keep up with traffic and then, on a better impulse, throw on my blinker and pull onto the shoulder.

The car, Bea's rental, slows to a stop. I put it in park and rest my forehead on the steering wheel.

I sit like that for a few minutes, the car swaying every time traffic passes.

This is not dissimilar to my breakdown last year. A few frantic, panicked decisions and then I freeze up and question everything. This time is more abrupt, but the tightness in my chest and the flutter of my heartbeat scream at me to DO SOMETHING BUT I DON'T KNOW WHAT.

I grapple with the phone and press at the screen until I call Arlo.

"Hey, Charlie." His voice is even and businesslike, and I close my eyes knowing that he's been working to clean up this mess the best he can.

"Charlie?" He's worried now.

"I'm here. I don't know what to do," I croak out.

"Where are you?"

I don't bother lifting my head. "On the highway some-where north of the city."

"Tell me where you are. I'll be right there."

Arlo's with his own fucking family and here he is on Christmas Eve, offering to come find me. I belatedly realize that if I were in his shoes, I would be *really fucking worried* about me, especially since I'm on the side of the highway. He's been through this with me once before, and I can't believe I'm dragging him through it again.

I sit up and shake my head. Not that Arlo can see it. "Wait, don't."

Arlo is quiet while I take deep breaths, move the car seat back to give myself more room, and stare at the odometer.

13,729. 13,729. 13,729.

There're small things my therapist taught me, but they help.

Eventually, I calm down. Arlo has probably heard my heavy, measured breathing throughout this entire ordeal, and he's been waiting patiently.

"I'm here. I'm better," I say.

"Good. Talk to me more. You said you don't know what you're doing? Tell me what you're literally doing right now and how you got there."

Another coping mechanism.

I explain how after his call I left my family. I borrowed Bea's car and left her—and everyone else—extremely pissed at me. I drove halfway to the city before my brain caught up.

"What were you going to do when you got to the city?"

"Go to the office and . . . I don't know. Try to fix things."

Arlo goes quiet for a moment. "Fix things? How?"

"I don't know! Talk to someone at ImmUniverse, I guess. Talk to a lawyer. Call Tasha."

"None of that requires your office. You could have done those things with your family around you, supporting you.

And I highly advise you not to talk to anyone at ImmUniverse. And why would you want to?"

I'm silent for a beat too long.

"Charlie," Arlo says carefully. "The deal is over. Not formally, but you don't want to do this deal. I know you. This is not what you want anymore."

My chest gets tight again and I squeeze my eyes shut. I'm back where I started last year and in an even worse spot. My exit strategy has failed and I'm trapped again, my business an albatross of stress pulling me down. Any dreams I have of caring for my family, taking care of Bea . . . they're all gone. Or at least delayed an indeterminate amount of time.

When I can finally speak, my voice is hoarse and choked. "I wanted it so badly."

"I know you did. But don't sacrifice everything else for this, okay?"

I nod. He's right, of course. I feel dumb for not seeing it myself.

"Okay?" he repeats, and this time I say it out loud.

"Okay."

"Would it be helpful to review some of your other exit strategy options now, or do you need to get off the highway?"

I give a shaky laugh. "Can we do both?"

"Of course."

I run my hands down my face and square my shoulders. I press the gas pedal and speed up, merging back into traffic as Arlo and I talk through some options while I take the next exit.

25

BEA

Someone knocks on my door, and I look up from my laptop. "Come in," I call.

All three of my sisters poke their heads into the room. When their eyes land on me—with my laptop out, my tablet next to it, a notebook in my lap and a pen in my hand—their faces shift. Yvette grins, Naomi's eyes narrow, and Kayla sags and rolls her eyes.

"What are you doing?" Naomi puts her hands on her hips and glares down at me. It's not super effective because she has to bend over to look at me since I'm on the bottom bunk.

"There's been a bit of a situation," I say.

Yvette flops down onto the bed next to me, jostling my laptop and accidentally touching the screen of my tablet and closing a browser tab. "See? Workaholic."

I shake my head. "Something happened to Charlie."

"Well, I don't want to be callous, but yeah, obviously. We were all there," Kayla adds.

"No," I say, and click around on my laptop until I find the *WSJ* article.

My sisters crowd around me to read it. Despite the highly technical matter, the article is written for consumers, and I don't have to explain much to them. Eyebrows raise, even as they bicker over scrolling down to read more.

"Oh damn," Kayla says when Rivrse's name first comes up.

"Shit," Yvette says when they get to the part about breaching terms of service.

They get to the end of the article and Naomi blows out a breath. "So what does this"— she gestures at the article— "have to do with this?" Now her hand encompasses my notes and devices.

"This," I say, swallowing hard. *This is me burying myself in my work.* "Is me helping my boss with an idea."

"Are you going to explain it to us?" Yvette asks.

"Nope," I say. It's a half-baked idea that Nash and I have been texting about until he went to bed with one last message that said *Merry Christmas—don't work on this tomorrow. We'll talk more when we get back.*

Kayla backs up, sitting against the wall and crossing her ankles. Now that I know she's pregnant, I can kind of tell that she's showing.

"Hey." Her fingers snap to get my attention. "My eyes are up here." She makes the universal gesture.

Yvette and Naomi shift on my other side to sit against the wall too. We move my work stuff around so I can sit back too. We're all still in our reindeer pajamas, feet hanging off the edge of the mattress.

Naomi rests her head on my shoulder. "Charlie wouldn't do that, right? The customer data stuff?"

Nash asked me the same thing—did I think Charlie was involved? It took me longer to answer Nash, but now I'm pretty sure.

"No, I don't think he would." Now that I understand what happened, I look back on this morning differently. Charlie wasn't leaving because he wanted to. He was leaving because he was *crushed*. Everything he'd worked for was gone in an instant.

I'm still mad at him. Why wouldn't he just tell me? Did he think I wouldn't understand? Or that I'd beg him not to go?

I pinch the bridge of my nose as tears finally, *finally,* try to break their way out. Of course, I would have begged him not to go. That's exactly the dynamic we had eight years ago. I was literally begging Charlie not to forget about me, not to leave me behind.

Or would I have? The girl I was back then doesn't exist anymore. I have a job I'm proud of, and having that self-worth makes a world of difference. I'm not desperately saving money or working a shitty job.

My sisters lean against me. Nash called me his friend, and when I told him I didn't think Charlie was involved, he trusted me, no questions asked.

The me from eight years ago wouldn't have had the courage to speak up about it.

There's another knock on the door. Mom, probably.

"Come in," I call.

The door swings open and Charlie steps in.

26

CHARLIE

smiles sneakily at me and Naomi gives me the stink eye.

I sit down on the bed opposite Bea, careful not to bump my head on the top bunk. Now that her sisters are gone, I can see that there's a laptop, a tablet, handwritten notes, and two smartphones on the bed.

Bea has been busy.

"Read the article, I guess?" It comes out almost a rasp.

The look she gives me is more sympathetic than anything else. But there's still anger there, aimed, deservedly, at me.

"Yeah." She stacks her things together and scoots to the edge of the bed, planting her feet on the floor and mirroring me.

My hands are sweating and I run my palms over my jeans before knotting my fingers together and resting my elbows on my knees. "There are some things I need to tell you."

Bea waits.

"We had a letter of intent to sell Rivrse to ImmUniverse."

Her eyes widen.

"I didn't tell you for a few reasons. One was that I'd signed an NDA. The other was that I wanted to surprise everyone. I didn't even tell my parents. And I think that the stress of it was wearing on me even more because of that.

"I'm selling Rivrse because the stress of a rapidly expanding business is not doing good things to me. Arlo, my mentor, helps a lot. So does my therapist. But I put a lot of pressure on myself, both just running the business and keeping it afloat while also trying to leave it in better hands with someone else." I laugh with no humor. "Unfortunately, the hands I picked were worse ones. All of this is to say, I'm sorry I left. I'm sorry I panicked and didn't think about anything other than myself."

"Yourself and everyone who works for you," Bea points out. "I read the article. I talked to Nash."

I close my eyes. Her wildly successful boss, a man whose career I admire, probably thinks I'm responsible for everything the article accuses me, or at least, my company, of.

"I didn't misuse data."

"I know," she says.

She says it so fast that I have to pause. Arlo didn't even ask—he knows everything there is to know about my business, almost knows it as well as I do. He gives me his support, always, and for that I'm thankful.

But there's something different about Bea saying it.

My eyes water and I look down, pinching the bridge of my nose and willing tears not to fall. She has faith in me, even after I drove away from her.

"I'm so sorry I left." I feel like I can't say the words enough. "I'll make it up to you."

Out of the corner of my eye, I see Bea stand and make her way over to me. She perches on the bed and rests her hand on my thigh. "I know you will. And I'm glad you came back. It would have been nice, though," she says, a hint of tease in her voice, "if you'd just never left in the first place."

I raise my arm and pull her into my side, kissing the top of her head. "There's something else I should tell you. Remember the summer I went to my grandma's house?"

"Yeah." Bea curls closer into me, like she knows what's coming, even though the only people I've ever talked to about this are Arlo, my therapist, and my parents.

"That was after dad got laid off, and we moved away from you. I loved my grandma, but she was a complicated woman. That summer all she could talk about was my parents' troubles, especially with money. She never liked that my mom worked as a waitress, and she said a lot of nasty things about . . ." I sigh. It's hard to say, even all these years later. "She said my mom was draining my dad, and she was going to leave him."

Bea's arm wraps around me and squeezes me tight.

"I didn't realize how much that fucked me up. And I'm working on it. But I'm terrified that someday I'll be on the other side of that story. I'll be the one sending my kid away and fighting about money."

"Have you talked to your parents about it?" Bea's whisper comes from somewhere next to my heart.

"Yeah. Years later. Mom cried and Dad was upset, but in that way that is really him upset with himself. They told me that their relationship troubles *were* about money, but it was *more* about Dad's rejection and his loss of self-worth." My therapist had gently pointed out that just because my grandmother had been an adult didn't mean that I should take what she said as truth. By the time I'd worked all this out, I went through a whole grief period of being angry at my grandmother, who, at that point, was already gone.

I hold Bea, and she holds me, and, after a few minutes, the thoughts of my company, my parents, and my grandmother fade away, so it's just me and Bea together.

"There's one more thing."

Bea stills, bracing herself for another painful memory or a more uncertain future.

"I love you," I say. "I don't expect you to say it back to me, because I was a colossal dick to you today, but you make me feel hope and joy and love even on one of the shittiest days of my life. And I promise, from now on, I will turn to you when I need to feel those things, even if it's hard and even if you don't want to give them to me. I *have* changed. Maybe not enough, but I want to keep working on it here with you."

Bea leans back and looks up at me, eyes shining. "I'll be here."

27

BEA

AFTER SUCH A HEAVY DAY, I CAN'T EVEN THINK ABOUT GETTING up. Charlie and I lay on the bed, just holding each other.

Charlie's the most driven person I know, and hearing his biggest fears—some of which have come to pass today—makes my heart ache for him.

I knew his summer with his grandmother had been rough. I'd heard it in his voice every time we talked on the phone. First, there was anger at his parents for sending him away for the summer, and then there was anger at his grandmother and a general anger at the world. He had come back different. I'd taken it to be that he was ready for his independence, to graduate and go to college and make his own life decisions.

Charlie sweeps a hand over my hair and presses his lips to my forehead. I'm glad he's back, but I still have questions.

"What's the plan now?" I ask, my heart fluttering in my chest. I can understand Charlie's actions, but where does that leave us? What does his future look like?

Charlie takes his lips off my skin and the point of his chin rests on my head. "Arlo and I have a few ideas that we haven't explored yet. He reminded me on my drive back—repeatedly—that selling to ImmUniverse was a strategic sale.

157

They wanted my business and my product. There are potential buyers or investors who would look at the sale from a financial perspective. The right buyer would do a better job of growing the company than I would. There are people who do that for a living—take a small-to-midsized business and buy it from the founder and scale it up to another sale or an IPO. And we haven't even discussed a sale with my staff and doing something like a management buyout, though I think that's less likely."

Nash had asked me a lot of questions about Charlie and Rivrse, many of which I couldn't answer. He wants to talk about it again after the holidays, but I don't really know to what end. It's probably not worth bringing up to Charlie right now.

"But," Charlie continues, "ultimately, what it comes down to is that I still have a huge commitment to my company. I work a lot. And it's stressful and hard and there are times when it's debilitating. But I want to get out of it. Maybe someday I'll start a new project, but I've learned a lot from this one, and I can make a better exit strategy from the beginning. I also have savings, and I want to start a family someday. It's not the security I wanted, but"—Charlie rolls us slightly so he's leaning over me, my shoulder brushing the wall—"I'm realizing that doesn't matter as much as I thought it did."

"No, it doesn't," I agree.

And then Charlie kisses me. It's slow and careful; loving. Just when I put my fists in his shirt to pull him over me and deepen it, my phone buzzes. It's extra loud because my phone has gotten wedged between the wall and the bunk bed, and Charlie lifts off me so I can rescue it.

There's a text from Naomi.

NAOMI

Um, are you guys done up there? We still need to do the family pictures.

"Well, as much as daydreaming about the future is fun, this Christmas is not over yet." I show him the text. "It's time to put on your pajamas again."

———

WE DO THE FAMILY PICTURES, INCLUDING ONE OF ME AND Charlie together. Charlie and I serve as judges for the snowman-building contest, which kept our families occupied while Charlie and I sorted ourselves out. Jasper's snowman is peeing into the woods, while Naomi's snowman wears her stethoscope (which she inexplicably packed for vacation). Susan's snowman is wearing a cape of some kind, and she tells us it's an effigy to Skadi, the Norse goddess of winter. Mom and Dad made a pair of snowmen holding hands, which Charlie and I, motivated by our reunion, chose as the winner.

Jasper roasts a turkey for dinner. Afterward we hang out in the living room, my pregnant sister on her back, head in Jasper's lap, while he has a protective hand on her belly. I think she's fallen asleep. Charlie and his parents disappear at some point and must have a long, wearing conversation, because he comes back tired and needing cuddles.

When we go back upstairs, I grab my things from the room I shared with Naomi and "move" into Charlie's room. Charlie is brushing his teeth while I check my phone.

There's a picture from Brin—she and Marco are posing with a snow person wearing a sundress and sunglasses. I double tap it to heart it.

The door opens and Charlie comes in, hair damp from the shower and breath minty-fresh, and strips before crawling into bed with me.

"Who are you texting?"

"My roommate Brin."

"The woman I met?"

I grimace. "I don't think I actually introduced you."

He chuckles and pulls me closer to him. "I'll make a better second impression. I can't wait to meet your friends."

"They're—"

I cut myself off. Why was I about to deny being friends with them? Unexpectedly, tears form in my eyes. Brin's so sweet, and maybe I've been doing them a disservice. Instead of being worried about being a messy roommate, maybe I should worry about being a better friend to them.

Nash's words echo in my head too.

Friends.

I turn my face to Charlie. "Who are your friends?"

He props his head up on his hand. "I have a few friends from college who are in New York now. I've seen them a couple of times since I've opened the office. And there's Arlo, who's probably one of my best friends. And mentor, and investor, and sometime—more frequently than I'd like—therapist. And one of my sales managers moved from the Bay Area to head the team in New York. You'd like her." He laughs. "There's also a programmer who used to work for me who recently reached out and we grabbed a coffee."

"They *used* to work for you? And you're still friends?"

He sighs. "I've made a lot of employment mistakes in the past. Most of them don't end well, and it's hard for either side not to take it personally. Arlo says I have to make the best decisions for Rivrse and see how things fall. Most of them don't resurface, but this one did. She's wildly talented and clever, but she wasn't a great fit. So, yeah, I'd call her a friend."

"Hmm. How would you feel about moving out of the city?" I'm not even sure I want to anymore. I definitely think Here is too small for me, but I want to leave my options open.

He doesn't hesitate. "Amazing. After I leave Rivrse," he amends.

I look up and pretend to give it a good, hard think. "After

you leave Rivrse. And kids?" I think I know how he feels about this from conversations back when we were teenagers. But I'm finding that there's a lot about Charlie that's changed.

He kisses my lips again before agreeing. "Lots of kids. How would you feel about me buying my parents a house?"

I snort. "How do they feel about it?"

Charlie breaks into a smile. "I'm working on it."

I laugh and he cuts it off with a kiss. This one's deeper, surer. And full of hope. So full it swells inside me and breaks through. "I love you too," I whisper against his lips when he lets me breathe.

This small town might have brought me exactly what I needed—and shown me what I already have.

28

BEA

It's a Christmas miracle—a day late, but there's an open parking spot right in front of my building. We unload my bags and Charlie helps me carry my stuff upstairs. It's late in the afternoon the day after Christmas, since we lingered as long as we could with our family before they had to leave for their flights in Albany. We're just going to drop my stuff off and say hi to Brin and Marco before I drive over to Charlie's. He wants to show me his new place and I'll stay the night tonight.

I have the next week off—the Heartly offices are mostly closed between Christmas and New Year's, and Nash is still out of town. Charlie asked me to show him around the city, and I've come up with an agenda: ice-skating at Rockefeller Center, snowman building after a fresh snowfall in Central Park, drinks at my favorite bar, and a colleague at Heartly invited me to a New Year's Eve party. I also asked Clara for restaurant recommendations, though I apologized for bothering her on her vacation.

"Please," she'd said. "If there's one thing I adore about living in the city, it's being my friends' go-to person for the best food recs. Now, have you been to that Javanese place I told you about?"

I unlock the door, swinging it open and striding down the hallway to the living room. "I'm home!"

There's a crash to my right and I glance over just in time to see a flash of skin and Brin and Marco's bedroom door closing.

Charlie and I glance at each other. And then I catch sight of the living room. There's pillows and blankets all over the place, like someone made a nest on the floor.

"Everyone okay in there?" I call out, officially worried about my roommates.

"Yup, just fine." Brin's voice is high and muffled. I hear some hushed whispering, and exchange a glance with Charlie.

I gently knock on the door. "We'll just be a few minutes and then I'm going to Charlie's."

Marco answers, "You don't have to go, Bea."

"I want to. I'll text you, but I'll be back tomorrow."

Charlie nudges me. "One night?"

"Or maybe in a few days."

Charlie laughs and follows me to my bedroom. He looks around, politely ignoring my mess and zoning in on the framed photographs of my family on the dresser, including one of the pajama pictures with his family from last year, and pictures from Kayla and Jasper's wedding.

I quickly throw my dirty clothes out of my luggage and toss clean ones in. I don't bother shouting goodbye to Brin and Marco, though I do hear murmured voices through their door.

"So, how long have your roommates been sleeping together?" Charlie asks me as we get back into the car, laughter in his voice.

"This is the first I've heard of it, so I'm guessing it'll be a very good story," I say.

"More epic than ours?" he says.

I tilt my head while I pull into traffic, thinking of how this story didn't just span this year's holiday but all the Christmases past. And it's changed the course for every Christmas that's yet to come.

"No, ours is definitely more epic."

EPILOGUE

Bea

Seven months later . . .

Charlie texts me fifteen minutes before his meeting with Nash.

> CHARLIE
>
> I'm on my way up.

> BEA
>
> See you soon!

This meeting has been in the works for months now, and it's been difficult having a conflict of interest. Obviously, Nash knows that I'm stuck in the middle, but we've been managing expectations.

Since the blowup over Christmas, Charlie was pretty disheartened about Rivrse. Our new relationship was a great distraction, but it was only temporary. After the start of the new year, Charlie had to dig into work again. I knew it was going to be hard, but it helped that I stayed at his place more often than mine, and I also had a deepening friendship with Marco, Brin, and some of her friends from the restaurant.

In the distance, I hear the elevator ding and stand. I pluck the half-frozen bottle of water from my desk and stop at the door to Nash's office. "Charlie's here. I'll send him in soon, okay?"

Nash smiles. "Sounds good."

I walk toward the elevator and intercept Charlie in the hallway. His smile blooms when he sees me. "Hey."

"Hey yourself. You look great." He does. His suit is a crisp dark gray, his tie a subtle green, and his briefcase is a soft, buttery leather that I know because I picked it out myself for his birthday present this year. I put a hand on his chest, beneath his tie, where I can feel his fluttering heart and the heat he radiates. Summers in New York can be rough, and I'm sure the combination of his nerves and the July heat are equally responsible for the slight dampness I feel.

"Come here," I say, and pull him into an empty conference room. I hand him the cold bottle. "Here, drink this."

Charlie's anxiety has been through the roof too, and I've learned to recognize the signs and what things I can do when he's struggling. He forgets to hydrate often, and in this heat, he needs it even more.

He chugs the bottle, taking long pulls until the ice clunks against the plastic. "Thank you," he gasps. Then he holds the icy bottle to his forehead.

"You're going to do great, okay? And it's Nash. You like him, he likes you." In addition to spending more time with Brin and Marco, I've also spent some time with Nash and Clara. Socially, anyway. Away from the office. Charlie has met Nash a few times, but this is all business today.

"Have I told you lately how wonderful you are?" he says.

"You can tell me again."

A grin pulls at his mouth. He pushes his nerves aside as he backs me up against the wall and grabs my chin, tilting my lips up to meet his. The kiss is deep and a little messy as our teeth clack together.

A throat clears behind us. Whoops.

Charlie steps back and laughs when he sees Arlo, who must have come up in the elevator a minute or two after Charlie, in the doorway.

He apologizes to his mentor, who just grins. "Whatever it takes to get your head in the game."

I like Arlo *a lot*. He's supported Charlie so much through the years and I'm glad he and Nash are finally meeting—I think they have a lot in common.

Charlie lets me lead them to Nash's office. Nash stands and greets them with handshakes and offers them a seat on the couch. I offer all three of them one last wave and close the door.

———

Charlie

Two hours later, I walk out of Nash's office in a bit of a daze. Bea gives me a hug, and whispers in my ear that we can talk about it tonight. She hugs Arlo goodbye too, and we leave Heartly's offices.

This time, when I step out on the streets of Manhattan, I want to shout for joy. The past seven months have been a trial, and while I'm still not where I thought I'd be, I can see the light at the end of the tunnel.

I turn to Arlo. "You don't think that's too good to be true, do you?" I ask.

His smile might just be brighter than mine. "It's definitely true. We don't know if it'll pan out yet, but it's the best offer we've had in a while."

It's the best offer we've had since ImmUniverse, he means. Which, in retrospect, wasn't a great offer.

This offer, while for less money than the previous one, sounds much better; a venture capital firm and Nash have partnered with an offer for Rivrse. Arlo knows someone on the VC board, and through Bea, I know Nash. He won't be involved in Rivrse after the sale, but he's taking a risk and putting money into its future success.

Legal troubles with ImmUniverse took some time. A big social media company filed separate lawsuits against Rivrse and ImmUniverse, with the lawsuit against Rivrse eventually being dropped, in part because, with the help of an expensive legal team, I filed my own suit against ImmUniverse. It's a massive liability to take on, but if Rivrse can win or settle, that will help repair our reputation. It also helped that Heartly didn't sue Rivrse.

"Charlie!" a voice calls from behind me. I turn around and Bea is dashing up the street as fast as her heels can carry her. I stride forward to meet her and she leaps into my arms. "You did so well," she says, voice muffled into my lapel. "You impressed Nash. He sent me home to celebrate with you."

I squeeze her once before letting go. "Do you want to go to The Plaza to celebrate?" I'm still learning the city, but I recently asked Brin what the best place to propose would be, and she gave me a list of options like:

Cheesy—top of the Empire State Building
Old-School Classy—The Plaza
Like a Tourist—Times Square complete with billboard
Public—the High Line

Private—Le Bernardin
Whimsical—Coney Island
Manicured Nature—St. Luke's in the Fields
Practical—Tiffany & Co.

There was a star next to private, which I took as a giant hint. I have a reservation for August 16 for a private room at Le Bernardin.

Bea pulls away and looks at Arlo. "What do you think? You want a drink?"

"I'm going to celebrate by going home to the family." He gives me a backslapping hug and Bea a kiss on the cheek before walking in the opposite direction toward the subway.

"Hmm," Bea says, looking up at me with a sparkle in her eyes. "What shall we do to celebrate?"

It takes us twenty minutes to get to my place, and another minute to get her bent over the kitchen counter, her skirt rucked up over her ass, her panties around one ankle, and me on my knees behind her. I strip off my button-up and fling it toward the door, where my jacket and tie litter the floor. I use my hands to pull her ass cheeks apart and dive in, savoring the way she tastes and the noises she makes as I pull her clit into my mouth and suck.

Bea gasps and writhes on the cool marble counter, and I get her right up to the edge before pulling away.

"What are you—" Bea raises her head, but I stand behind her, unbuckling my belt and pulling out my cock. Bea makes a whimpering sound of anticipation and I line myself up, pants around my ankles.

When I slide inside her, it feels so good, like home. I regret having an eight-year gap in our relationship when we weren't doing this as often as we could, but we both needed to grow in our own ways. Our relationship would have broken one way or another, and I can't see how it could have come back together so perfectly any other way.

I reach out and pluck at the golden coil of Bea's hair. "Undo it," I rasp. She reaches back to pull out the three pins that hold her hair in place, and when it twirls loose I thread my fingers through it and hold her to the counter. "Grab the other side."

She reaches her arms up to grip the edge of the counter and brace herself. I put my other hand on the small of her back, enough that she feels pinned, and I begin thrusting.

Her hands don't stay on the beveled edge long. I'm taking her hard, and she scrambles, getting desperate with each slap of our bodies.

I come as she calls out my name, and as soon as I catch my breath, I drop back to my knees. I swipe my tongue over her slit again and taste both of us combined. Fuck, that's hot. I alternate between sucking and licking until her right foot, still in her work heels, trembles and lifts off the floor, her toes curling as she pulses her orgasm against my face.

I keep licking without touching her clit, slowly and carefully letting her come down until she moans in sweet satisfaction.

Finally, I rise and curl over her back, kissing her spine right above the edge of her sleeveless blouse.

She groans and I help her slip off the counter. She tilts her head back and laughs. "Well, that was one way to celebrate."

"Water?" I offer.

"Yes, please."

I pull my pants up and button them so they don't fall down again, and fetch us both a glass and some cool water from the fridge dispenser. My eye catches on the magnet I bought her for Christmas—"I Love Doodles."

I smile when I pass her the water, remembering that night by the Christmas tree.

"What?" she says, eyes curious. I gesture at the magnet, and she chuckles.

While I don't know where this deal is going to take us, I'm less worried about where my life is going now.

It's going to be a Bea-utiful life.

The End

Want one more sexy scene with Bea and Charlie at next year's Christmas? Scan the QR code to sign up for my newsletter for an exclusive bonus chapter.

Please Review
Reviews are critical to all authors. You can leave a review for
Ghost of Ex-mas Past at
your preferred retailer and at
Goodreads and BookBub.

For a list of Liz Alden's books, please visit
lizalden.com/books

ACKNOWLEDGMENTS

This year has been one of the most hectic years of my life, and it's no surprise that I yearn for something a little simpler. Maybe even some wish fulfillment.

Writing *Butter You Up,* a book in the Farm 2 Forking shared series, opened a door for me to peer into small-town romances and everything that comes with them . . . and SURPRISE! That door doesn't want to close. Kit and Here elbowed their way into my brain and wouldn't shut up. I had to set this book in Here and give Kit a guest appearance. He'll get his own romance soon, as will more inhabitants of the town of Here.

As for me, I expect to fall in love with my own little small town soon.

Thank you to Sara Whitney, Lainey Davis, and Karen Grey for reading early versions of this book and making thoughtful suggestions. Thank you also to Annette Szlachta, my proofreader.

And as always, a big thank-you to my husband, who encouraged me so much from day one, and my parents, all five of them, who supported this book in one way or another.

ABOUT LIZ ALDEN

Liz Alden is a digital nomad. Most of the time she's on her sailboat, but sometimes she's in Texas. She knows exactly how big the world is—having sailed around it—and exactly how small it is, having bumped into friends worldwide.

She's been a dishwasher, an engineer, a CEO, and occasionally gets paid to write or sail.

The books are inspired by her real-life travel.

Follow Liz:

www.ingramcontent.com/pod-product-compliance
Lightning Source LLC
Chambersburg PA
CBHW021710190726
48289CB00008B/2460

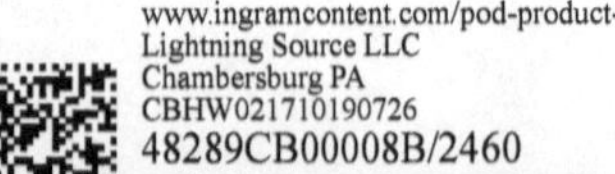